Richard Wagner, Charles Tindal Gatty, Amherst Webber

**The Sacred Festival-Drama of Parsifal**

Richard Wagner, Charles Tindal Gatty, Amherst Webber

**The Sacred Festival-Drama of Parsifal**

ISBN/EAN: 9783337334550

Printed in Europe, USA, Canada, Australia, Japan

Cover: Foto ©Andreas Hilbeck / pixelio.de

More available books at **www.hansebooks.com**

# *THE SACRED FESTIVAL-DRAMA*

OF

# PARSIFAL,

BY

RICHARD WAGNER.

THE ARGUMENT, THE MUSICAL DRAMA, AND THE MYSTERY,

BY

CHARLES T. GATTY, F.S.A.

---

Je ne sais qu'une chose plus belle que *Parsifal*, c'est n'importe quelle messe basse dans n'importe quelle Eglise."—ALFRED ERNST.

---

*LONDON:*
SCHOTT AND CO.,
157 & 159, REGENT STREET.

[*The Editors' translation of the text of the Drama, and the musical themes from the pianoforte score, are both embodied in this work by consent of Messrs. Schott & Co., who are the owners of the copyrights and right of translation in the poem and music.*]

[*For the translation of the Libretto, and the supervision of the musical portion of this volume, the writer is indebted to Mr. Amhurst Webber. He has also to acknowledge many valuable suggestions from Lieut.-Col. Ewing.*]

# PARSIFAL.

## The Argument.

### The Holy Grail and the Brotherhood of Knights.

ONCE on a time, when the domain of the true faith was threatened by the craft and power of pagan barbarians, there came down in the midst of holy night to the pious hero Titurel sacred messengers of the Lord Jesus, who gave into this good man's keeping that precious vessel, and most hallowed noble cup called the Holy Grail, out of which the Lord Himself drank at His last Feast of Love, and into which His precious Blood flowed when He hung upon the cross. And with this was also given the sacred Lance which shed that life-giving stream. To enshrine and guard these precious symbols of divine love, Titurel built a sanctuary called the Castle of Monsalvat among the mountains in the north of Spain, and gathered round him a brotherhood of knights. And to this community only the pure in heart were admitted, but to them was given, by the supernatural sustenance of the Grail, strength to do the highest and holiest deeds of Christian chivalry.

### Klingsor's Magic Castle and Kundry.

And many sought to become guardians of the Holy Grail, but could not because of their sins. Amongst these was Klingsor, who craved for the holier life, yet was not able to stem the tide of evil in his heart, and he was refused admission. Powerless to kill sin in his soul, he laid a guilty hand upon his body, and this hand he again stretched forth to grasp the Holy Grail ; but Titurel spurned him scornfully. Enraged at this, and discovering through his fury that his infamous act gave him the powers of magic, he used the enchantments of that diabolical craft to destroy the guardians of the Grail, and gain its custody. He transformed the desert beyond the Grail's domain into a wondrous garden of delight, peopled with beautiful women, and hither he allured many of Titurel's knights to their destruction. By the power of his sorcery he drew under the slavery of a magic spell the woman Kundry, once called Herodias, who mocked the Saviour as He went to Calvary, and was thenceforth doomed to carry her mocking laughter from existence to existence, and from world to world. Kundry was the chief instrument of Klingsor's envious revenge. In her mysterious personality she displayed a dual nature. In one phase she appeared in the Grail's domain as a wild witch-like being, the penitent, helpful, solicitous servant of the knights; and from this she was transformed, by means of a magic sleep, into a woman of surpassing beauty, the destructive seductress of Klingsor's enchanted garden.

### The Fall of Amfortas.

Now when king Titurel grew very old, he conferred the lordship of the Grail upon his son Amfortas, and he it was who resolved to make an end of the seductions of Klingsor's garden. Unmindful of the consecrated token, and full of pride at his own prowess, he presumed to arm himself with the sacred Lance and attack the enchanter's palace. But Klingsor had called Kundry to his aid, and to her beauty Amfortas yielded. Whilst he lay entranced in her arms, the Magician not only stole the Lance which had dropped unheeded from its guardian's hand, but plunged it into the young king's side, so that it was with difficulty that Gurnemanz, the faithful companion of Amfortas, covered his shameful flight from the enchanted castle. And now, puffed up by the possession of the holy weapon, Klingsor raised his ambitious hopes to the high expectation that the Grail itself would soon be his.

### The Repentance of Amfortas and the Prophecy.

Meanwhile Amfortas lingered on in the castle of Monsalvat, helpless and suffering, tortured by the wound which nothing would heal, and by a remorse which neither tears nor repentance would assuage. In vain he was carried each morning and bathed in the sacred lake, and in vain the knights sought far and near for herbs that would heal his wound. But the burning smart of his guilty conscience pierced deeper than the Lance which cleft his side, and when, by reason of his kingly office, there fell to him the duty of revealing the Holy Grail to the brotherhood, his torture was terrible to behold. He was filled with horror at the thought that upon him, the chief guardian of the Grail, whose perfect purity was lost, should fall the duty of unveiling to a community of chaste souls the most holy treasure upon earth. At the sight of the relic the blood gushed from his side. Such was the awful chastisement of an offended God for the sin of Amfortas. Helpless and despairing, the sinner turned to the Saviour for peace and hope. He prostrated himself before the plundered sanctuary, and in impassioned prayer begged for a sign of deliverance. And now, from out the glowing radiance of the Holy Grail, there shone forth the vision of One who spoke these prophetic words of promise :—

"By pity enlightened,
The stainless Fool :
Wait for him,
My chosen One."

Such was the message of hope and consolation given to Amfortas, and, though the knights of the Grail did not understand its full meaning, they lived in expectation of a deliverer.

## Parsifal the Deliverer.

And when the time came for the prophecy to be fulfilled, its hero Parsifal was born, far away in Arabia, where his father Gamuret had been killed in battle. And his mother Herzeleide, wishful to keep her child from the service of arms and fighting, brought the boy up among the moors and wood-lands, away from the haunts of men. But Parsifal grew up fierce and strong, and made for himself a bow and arrows to kill the wild eagles and defend him against savage beasts and giants. And, as he roamed through the forests, he met by chance with the knights of the Grail, "glittering men on beautiful animals," whom he longed to be like, and whom he followed, but could not overtake. And at last, to his mother's bitter grief, he wandered quite away and returned no more. He was about to fulfil the high mission for which he had been destined.

## How Parsifal came to the Grail's Domain.

It was at daybreak, on a lovely morning, that Parsifal wandered by chance into the domain of the Holy Grail, and found himself on the banks of the sacred lake in which king Amfortas, attended by knights, was then taking his daily bath. Over the waters circled a wild swan, whose snowy plumage glistened in the sunshine. Within these holy precincts all animal life was held sacred, so that Amfortas looked upon the bird's flight over his head as a fortunate omen. But Parsifal, who drew his bow at every flying thing, wounded the swan with an arrow, and the bird, fluttering towards the castle, fell through the trees dead near a group of knights who surrounded the culprit, and with cries of dismay hurried him to Gurnemanz the faithful armourer of the king. Bending over the dead creature, Gurnemanz asked the wanton boy how he could bring himself to murder this goodly bird which had never harmed him. The knight pointed to the arrow, the blood, the powerless pinions, and the look yet lingering in the failing eye. Parsifal listened attentively, at first with astonishment, and then with increasing emotion. Finally he broke the bow over his knee and flung it with the arrows upon the ground. When the knight asked him if he was conscious of his guilt, the boy drew his hand across his eyes, for the first rays of pain and pity had dawned upon his soul. Gurnemanz asked whence he came, and who sent him, but the boy knew nothing. He could not recall any of the many names he once had, and did not even know the name of his father. Gurnemanz thought to himself that this was the dullest dolt he had ever met with, excepting the witch-like woman Kundry who was lying on the ground close by. At the same time the old knight was impressed by the noble bearing of this youth, and being disposed to question him alone, he sent the young knights to assist Amfortas at his bath, and they reverently bore away towards the lake the body of the dead swan, laid upon a bier of green branches, leaving Gurnemanz and Parsifal alone, with Kundry watching near. The knight asked the boy to tell him what he *did* know. Parsifal replied that he knew his mother, Herzeleide. Kundry watched the youth with increasing interest, and spoke of his parentage and bringing up, the fear he inspired by his fierce spirit and strength. "Who fears me?" he cried. "The wicked," she replied. "Who is good?" he asked, to which Gurnemanz answered reproachfully, "Your mother, whom you deserted, and who grieves and laments for you." Then Kundry told them that his mother was dead, that she had seen her dying as she rode along, and brought him Herzeleide's blessing. The boy sprang upon the witch and seized her by the throat. This was his second revelation of pain, and it drove him to madness. The old knight separated them and expostulated with the violent youth. Whilst Parsifal stood trembling and nearly fainting, Kundry filled a horn with water at the brook, sprinkled his face, and gave him to drink. Gurnemanz commended this kindly act, which gave good for evil as the Grail commanded.

### Kundry is called away.

But Kundry turned sadly away saying "I never do good," and crept slowly towards the thicket like a hunted thing. Klingsor was calling to her. He saw that the promised deliverer was about to enter upon his mission, and needing the services of Kundry he drew her through the portal of sleep under the influence of his magic spell. He wanted her to effect Parsifal's ruin, not minister to his needs. All the good she tried to do was of no avail against the power of this spell. She had that day brought a phial of healing balsam to try to undo the terrible evil she had caused by her seduction of Amfortas. And now the sleep of sin began to fall over her again, and impelled her to work further destruction. She longed for rest—aye, for eternal sleep—for the deadly slumber of the magic spell terrified her soul as it crept over her. "Vain to resist" she murmured, sinking down behind the thicket; "vain to resist! The time has come! Sleep—sleep: I must!"

## Parsifal is called to the Hall of the Holy Grail.

And now the hour had arrived for Parsifal to be initiated into the mysteries of the Holy Grail. Providence had guided the steps of the innocent hero to his mighty destiny. He had not sought the Grail, for he did not know of its existence, and had wandered aimlessly into its domain. Indeed it was the guileless innocence of Parsifal's simple soul which had attracted the attention of Gurnemanz and aroused his curiosity. What if this were the stainless Simple One of the prophecy! The knight was eager to put him to the test. The excited and exhausted youth had been leaning on his support, and Gurnemanz now laid the boy's arm on his own neck and bore him gently along, saying he would conduct him to the Holy Feast, and that if he was pure the Grail would give him food and refreshment. Parsifal asked, "Who is the Grail"? The knight told him that he might not say, but that if he was to be called to its service, he would know. Indeed the knight betrayed his own dim prescience of Parsifal's high vocation by saying, "I think I have recognised you aright." And now the two moved gently onwards towards the castle. As they approached the sacred enclosure it seemed to Parsifal that he was borne along without effort. The forest glade around them disappeared, giving place to the ramparts of a mighty fortress. He turned to Gurnemanz and said, "I hardly step, and yet I seem already far," to which the knight replied, "You see, my son, that time here becomes space." In the spiritual environment material limitations were no more. They had entered the supernatural atmosphere surrounding the shrine of this sacred symbol of suffering, through which the unclean and the unwelcome could not pass. It was not given to every soul to penetrate the mystery of the Saviour's suffering. Only those who could share the tribulation and sympathise with the sorrow, should partake of the Sacred Feast. Gurnemanz led Parsifal up the ascending rock-hewn passages which rose from the foundations of the castle of

Monsalvat into the great hall of the Holy Grail. A loud blast of trumpets and the clang of deep bells were calling the brotherhood to the sacred ceremony. Parsifal found himself in a mighty hall surrounded by clusters of marble columns, and surmounted in the centre by a high dome under which was a stone table on a raised dais. In front were two half-circular refectory tables. When Gurnemanz had brought Parsifal into the hall and was about to leave him and join the rest of the brotherhood, he said to the boy, "Now pay attention, and if you are a fool, and pure, let me see what knowledge and wisdom may be given to you."

And now through doors at the end of the hall marched processions of knights, clad in pale blue tunics and scarlet cloaks embellished with the symbol of the Holy Spirit. The knights sang as they marched a hymn in praise of the divine gifts in the sacred Love Feast of the Lord. When the knights had taken their places at the refectory tables, their wounded king Amfortas was borne in upon a litter, whilst a choir of youths in the mid-height of the dome sang to a refrain of piercing sadness the readiness of the brotherhood to share the sorrows and sufferings of the Saviour. Before the king walked four esquires, one of them carrying under a draped cover the precious chalice of the Holy Grail, which was set before Amfortas upon the stone table; after which boys' voices from the extreme height of the dome burst into heavenly harmony. Parsifal stood gazing upon the scene, astonished and entranced. Amfortas was laid upon a couch behind the stone table under the dome, the knights took their places round the refectory tables, the harmonies in the height were hushed, and, amid a solemn stillness, the voice of king Titurel was heard commanding his son Amfortas to unveil the Grail. The aged monarch called from a chapel in the apse of the temple in which he rested entombed, pleading for the supernatural nourishment of the Grail by which his enfeebled frame was sustained. Amfortas half raised himself from his couch, and smarting with remorse, entreated his father to live on, re-assume the holy office, and let him perish. But Titurel pleaded that he was too old and feeble to serve his Lord, that Amfortas must seek forgiveness in good works and fulfil his duty by unveiling the Grail. The esquires advanced to uncover the precious chalice, but Amfortas motioned them back, and begged that it might be left unrevealed. In impassioned words he disclosed to the brotherhood the tortures inflicted by his guilty conscience. The pain of his wound was as nothing compared with the pangs of remorse provoked by the reflection that he, a vile sinner in a chaste community, should have inherited a sacred duty demanding the precious innocence he had lost. The Holy Grail, which to them was rapture and refreshment, to him was agony unutterable. His broken heart yearned for compassion, he longed to be forgiven. Gazing before him, as in a trance, he thought he beheld the Grail revealed, and the Precious Blood glowing in the crystal chalice. It seemed as if the sacred stream rushed into his heart, and for a moment stemmed the ever-advancing tide of his own iniquitous life-blood. Then back again coursed the sinful flood, out through the gaping spear wound. His soul then turned to Calvary, and he saw that other wound inflicted by the self-same Lance, which opened to the human race the Heart of infinite compassion. "Mercy! mercy! Thou all-merciful One," he cried aloud, "take mine inheritance, close the wound, that I may die holy, pure once more in Thy sight." As he sank back exhausted and unconscious upon the couch, softly, from out the extreme invisible height of the vast dome, came the sound of voices singing the prophecy of hope:—

"By pity enlightened,
The stainless Fool:
Wait for him,
My chosen One."

### The Glowing of the Grail.

Then the knights in the great hall caught up the strain, and called upon Amfortas to wait on in hope, but fulfil the duty before him, and the aged Titurel cried aloud, "Unveil the Grail." Amfortas raised himself slowly and painfully from his couch, whilst the young esquires removed the cover from the golden shrine, brought forth the ancient cup of pure rock crystal, and set it before the young king. From the height of the dome the voices sang, "Take unto you My Body, take unto you My Blood, the symbol of our love." As the young king bent in prayer over the Grail and the brotherhood knelt around, the temple became obscured by a marvellous gloom which gradually deepened into complete darkness. The air quivered with vibrations of mysterious music, the sacred chalice glowed blood-red, and a ray of blinding light shot from the summit of the dome upon the radiant features of Amfortas, who raised the holy relic, and moved it from side to side blessing the bread and the wine.

The voice of the aged king Titurel cried from his cell, "O celestial rapture, how glorious to-day is the salutation of the Lord!"

Then Amfortas set down the Holy Grail upon the table, and the gloom waned as the daylight once more filled the hall. And the knights being again seated at the tables, the bread and wine were given to each in turn. Then Gurnemanz beckoned to Parsifal that he should come and occupy a vacant place at his side, and share in the Feast of Love, but the boy stood, apparently unconscious and dumbfounded. On hearing the strong cry of agony uttered by Amfortas, Parsifal had clutcned at his own heart, as if to repress the torture of an overwhelming sympathy. He now stood rigid, like one in a dream, whilst the boys' voices chanted a hymn in praise of the Body and the Blood, and the knights, having partaken of the bread and wine, joined in the sacred strain as they rose from the table, embraced each other, and marched from the hall in solemn procession. Parsifal saw Amfortas carried forth by the esquires, his head bowed upon his breast, his hand pressed against the wound which had burst out afresh; and when Amfortas had gone, the boy stood as if petrified, absolutely alone in the great hall. Then Gurnemanz returned, and taking Parsifal by the arm, shook him petulantly and asked him why he stood there, and if he comprehended what he had seen. Parsifal said nothing, but only shook his head, and clutched at his heart. The old knight turned upon him angrily and opening a door at the side, exclaimed; "You are after all then nothing but a Fool! Get out there, go your own way! But Gurnemanz advises you: in future leave our swans in peace, and gander as you are, seek a goose for yourself!" He then thrust the boy out and slammed the door after him.

As Gurnemanz turned to recross the hall and follow the knights, a mysterious voice echoed from the height of the dome,

"By pity enlightened, the stainless Fool."

## Klingsor Awakes Kundry.

Now Klingsor feared the stainless simplicity of Parsifal, and set himself to rob the guileless youth of purity and life, by devilish machinations. Conscious of the prophecy, and knowing that Parsifal had entered the Grail's domain, the Magician had already anticipated the issue by calling Kundry through the medium of the magic sleep. Kundry was to lure the victim into her arms, and Klingsor would then kill him with the sacred Lance.

Seated within the inner keep of his fortress, surrounded by the appliances of his craft, the Magician eagerly watched in his magic mirror the approach of the daring boy. There was no time to be lost, so he hastened to awaken Kundry from her enchanted slumber. He kindled a mystic flame out of which came forth a blue vapour, and having reseated himself before the magic mirror passed the mysterious gestures of necromancy over the depth, and called upon Kundry to arise. And there, in the midst of a weird light which permeated the cloud of vaporous blue, appeared the form of a beautiful woman, as if asleep. Presently she moved, and then awakened with a cry of horror. At the derisive greeting of her magic master she uttered another shriek of anguish, which died away in a wail of terror. Then did the Magician taunt her with roving in the Grail's domain where she was regarded as a wild beast, whereas with him she received honour, since she had seduced the chief guardian of the Grail. But Kundry called in broken accents for the sleep of death. She spoke of her services to the Grail knighthood, which Klingsor told her were of no avail since every man of them had his price, and even the firmest were weak. He then reminded her that on that day she was about to encounter the most dangerous of all, whose shield was foolishness. In this half-awakened state reminiscences of her better self lingered in her heart, and she tried to resist the magic spell, and refuse the Magician's commands. When she asked him by what power he could enforce them, he actually appealed to his being proof against her charms, as if this were derived from a virtuous resistance instead of an infamous degradation. With a fiendish laugh she cried out to him, "*Art thou chaste?*" Stung to the quick by her mocking taunt, then poisoned by the recollection that he had once sought the holier life and failed to gain it, the apostate boasted of his power, and warned her that he had already overthrown Amfortas, acquired the sacred Lance, and would soon be master of the Grail. But Kundry pleaded only for release in the eternal sleep of death, on which Klingsor reminded her that the man who resisted her charms would set her free, and mockingly recommended that she should try her fortune with the approaching boy. Then hastily mounting the tower wall he blew upon a horn a note of warning to the garrison below, and surveyed with keen appreciation the coming of Parsifal. The spectacle of a high-mettled boy, all aglow with the vigour of healthy youth, scaling ramparts and battlements, and cutting to pieces their enervated and effeminate defenders, excited genuine admiration in the belligerent Magician. He shouted with satanic laughter as Parsifal wrested the arms from the hero Ferris and severed the limbs of his impotent supporters. On turning round to tell Kundry that the time had come, he found her gone. With wild hysterical laughter ending in a cry of anguish, she had vanished into darkness.

### Parsifal comes into the Enchanted Garden.

Meanwhile Parsifal, who had been ignominiously thrust out of the Castle of the Grail, came along shouting with delight at the sight of Klingsor's enchanted towers. With fierce courage he scaled the ramparts of the fortress, killing or disabling any of the garrison who resisted his approach. He soon found himself in the enchanted garden of the magic domain on which he stood gazing with childlike amazement, his eyes dazzled by the garish splendour of its rank luxuriant vegetation. Before him opened a tangled grove of tropical trees and creepers, laden with huge gorgeous flowers which blazed in the brilliant sunshine. And now there ran into this grove from all sides, first singly, then in groups, beautiful maidens, uttering cries of lamentation over their dead or disabled lovers, whom Parsifal had overthrown upon the ramparts. They rushed about in confusion, bewailing their beloved, clamouring for vengeance, and calling out for the culprit. When they caught sight of Parsifal standing on the wall, with the reddened sword of the hero Ferris still in his hand, they recognised him as their enemy, and heaped reproaches and curses upon him. Then he flung away the weapon and leaped down the terraces towards them, but the maidens shrank from him asking how he dared to approach them after slaying their lovers. But when he praised their beauty, excused his violence as necessary in order to come to them, said he meant them no hurt, and in innocent wonder offered to play with them, then they crowded round him, and competed with each other for his attentions. They ran off in companies to dress themselves up like flowers, and came back in turn, dancing round him to a slow seductive melody, singing:—"Come! Come! You bonny boy! Come! Come! Let me bloom for you! Come! To your pleasure and delight will I devote all my loving efforts!" They tendered him kisses and caresses, they reproached him for his coldness, they quarrelled and clamoured for him, they crowded closer and closer about him, and hustled each other to monopolize him, until he pushed them crossly away and was about to fly, when suddenly a strange voice called aloud, "Parsifal! Stay!"

### Kundry.

The startled maidens stood back, and Parsifal turned in astonishment towards an arbour in the grove from whence the voice proceeded. "Parsifal"—yes—he remembered then that his mother once called him by that name in her dream. How strange to hear it again in that enchanted garden from lips that bade him stay to feast on joy and gladness!

The voice then bade the crowd of frivolous wanton girls to go and tend their wounded lovers, and as they retired into the castle, reluctant and complaining, they cried out derisively to Parsifal, "Farewell! You fair one! You proud one! You—Fool!"

Parsifal now turned shyly in the direction from which the voice had come, and saw, emerging from a bower of tropical foliage the vision of Kundry, transformed into a young woman of surpassing beauty, reclining upon a floral couch. It seemed to Parsifal as if he were in a dream. Was it him she had called, him who had no name? Yes, and she repeated it again, told him how Gamuret his father had thus styled him before ever he was born, and how she herself had come from far and tarried long only to call him "Parsifal."

### Parsifal's first temptation, and the kiss of Kundry.

With tender emotion she spoke to him of his mother Herzeleide, of her love and care for him as a little child, when he was the one joy of her widowed heart. She pictured him as he lay nestled on her bosom, laughing in blissful love, the delight of her eyes and the solace of her sadness. She recalled how Herzeleide watched over the boy's childhood, how she reared him far away from men in the wild country, amid the mossy moorlands and forests, where he should never know of arms or learning, lest he should inherit his father's violent fate. She reminded him how he roamed away from his mother's side, at first only for the tiny excursions of infant feet, when she ran after him and brought him back laughing, but later on with the more ambitious expeditions of impatient youth, eager for adventure, when he wandered beyond her power of recall. And then she told him that when he left his mother, and she could find no trace of him, Herzeleide waited for a while, and then gradually pined away, and died of a broken heart.

With consummate art the temptress Kundry began her diabolical work by an appeal to Parsifal's one experience of love, with which she craftily simulated a woman's genuine sympathy. No nearer way to his heart could have been chosen. Unmanned by an overwhelming compunction, and overcome by sorrow and remorse at his own cruel indifference to his mother's love, Parsifal sank down at the feet of the seductress, unconscious of the net spread for his destruction. He accused himself of being his mother's murderer, reproached himself for his neglect, folly and forgetfulness, and falling into an almost vacant state of despondency, yielded to the sympathetic endearments of Kundry, who bent over him, and inviting him to experience the love of Gamuret and Herzeleide, twined her arms confidingly around his neck, and pressed her lips upon his mouth in a long passionate kiss—the last greeting of his mother's blessing, the first kiss of love!

## The Great Enlightenment.

The sensual shaft of her embrace pierced the stainless veil of his innocent soul, and stung him to the quick. Thrilled with the first intoxication of sinful desire, the guileless Fool tasted the fruit of the tree of knowledge of good and evil. For a moment he mistook the burning smart of Kundry's kiss for a real wound bleeding in his bosom. As this illusion passed away he recognised in the piercing pain the torment of transgression which he had seen burst forth from the heartbroken Amfortas in the Hall of the Holy Grail. He sprang to his feet with a gesture of intense terror, and clutching at his heart to repress the wild throbbing of its bewildering agony, cried out "Amfortas! The wound! The wound!" From the depths of his soul there went up a wail of lamentation, like the wail of the wounded king which rent the Hall of the Grail, an echo of the Wail of the crucified God. The hour of his great enlightenment had come. The kiss of Kundry had betrayed to him the secret source of human sin, the provocation of divine sorrow. The floodgates of his stainless heart were opened and there came forth a torrent of divine compassion for fallen man. His senses reeled, his eyes gazed into vacancy, he saw once more the sacred shrine and the gleaming Chalice of Christ's Blood, shedding the rapture of redemption from its heavenly radiance on all around. There rang through all his being the Saviour's Wail of lamentation for His polluted sanctuary, crying out to him, "Redeem Me, rescue Me from hands defiled by guilt!" An inspiration of the Great Renunciation then dawned upon his soul. He had felt commiseration for the dead swan, compunction for his mother's death, pity for Amfortas; and was now lifted up from particular human sympathies to the comprehension of divine universal compassion. Henceforth he would follow the Wail of God and co-operate with the aspirations and labours of Redeeming Love. In bitter despair at the random exploits of his past folly, he flung himself upon his knees and cried aloud:—"Redeemer! Saviour! Lord of Grace! How can I, a sinner, atone for my guilt?"

## Parsifal's Second Temptation.

During this passionate outburst Kundry watched Parsifal with awestruck wonder. She saw that at one bound he had crossed the chasm which divides an aimless innocent boy, from an enlightened, determined and heroic man. She no longer appealed to him through the medium of reminiscence, but brought all the armoury of her woman's physical beauty to bear direct upon him as a man. She crept up timidly to where he still knelt upon the ground, addressed him coaxingly as the promised hero, and begged him to fling away the delusions which filled his brain, and yield to the joys of love. She bent her body over him as he knelt, looked into his eyes, held her lips out towards his, leaned her neck against his head, allowed her hair to flutter over his face, and twined her arms around his neck. But Parsifal instinctively identified in every amorous endearment of the fallen woman, the occasion of the ruin of Amfortas. He saw in his mind's eye the tragedy of that temptation again enacted. With grim irony he designated every gesture of her fascination, fitting the word to the action. Finally, in an outbreak of angry derision, he accused her of kissing away with her lips the salvation of her victim ; and then rising to his feet he cast her away from him, crying out, "Corruptress! Away from me! For ever, for evermore away from me!"

## Kundry's Appeal for Pity.

With the inherent aptitude of the subtle feminine temperament to adapt itself to every aspect of an opponent, and anticipate every movement in a campaign, regardless of policy or consistency, yet acting under a genuine impulse towards apparent good, Kundry exchanged her seductive craft for an earnest appeal to Parsifal's pity. If he must sympathise with others let him have compassion on her. In a wild burst of supplication she pleaded her desire for redemption. He was the saviour for whom she had waited for an eternity. She told him of the curse which lay upon her, awake or asleep, in life or death, in pain or laughter. She pictured to him how when she met the Saviour bearing His Cross towards the hill of Calvary, she greeted Him with mocking laughter, and His look fell upon her! She told how from that moment she had wandered forth, the victim of convulsive laughter, ever seeking the Saviour from world to world, to beg one glance of pity. At times it seemed to her as if His eye were near, then back came the accursed laughter, as a sinner sank into her arms! Weep she could not, only laugh, laugh, grovel, and rage, in wild unending delirium! All she craved was to weep, to sob for one brief hour upon the breast of her deliverer, and then, though outcast from God and man, in love for *him* her sins would be atoned, and she would be redeemed.

But all her supplications were in vain. The enlightened and immaculate comprehension of Parsifal, whose mission was now clear and determined, was proof against her spurious assurance of salvation through desire. He spurned the project which would have damned them both, and offered her redemption at the price of repentance. He told her that the consolation she sought sprang not from the fountain of carnal longing which welled up always in her heart, nor could it ever be attained till that polluted stream were staunched. Far different from this was the true balm of redemption for which the holy knights were craving. And though the mysteries of saving faith could only be apprehended as through a glass darkly by human souls, the blackest night of all worldly vanities was to seek salvation in the very spring-head of damnation!

### Kundry's Last Resource.

One other resource remained, and Kundry rushed to it in reckless despair. She had failed to win the hero through her simulated sympathy, or the fascination of her bodily beauty, or her appeal to his pity for her outcast state. From the fiery furnace of each temptation he had come forth victorious and unscathed. In action and in understanding Parsifal had proved himself a hero, endowed with a complete comprehension of Pity and Renunciation. She had put him to the proof, and he had proved his power. Nay more, he had proved himself *conscious* of his power, and an appeal to that consciousness was Kundry's last resource.

In wild exultation she turned to him saying that if her kiss had been the means of conveying such mighty knowledge to his soul, her embrace would assuredly transfigure him into a god. Then might he redeem the world, if he wished; and as for her, she would willingly sell her soul to hell to purchase his omnipotence! The impious suggestion fell sterile from her lips, and Parsifal again offered her deliverance if she would show him the way back to Amfortas.

### Kundry Curses Parsifal's Path.

The way back to Amfortas! This was more than Kundry could bear. Her hero might refuse her sympathy, resist her allurements, repudiate her appeal, and reject her arguments; this only made him in her estimation the better worth winning, whilst the very struggle reflected some credit on her capacity; but that he should ask her to show him the way back to a man she had regarded as a weak fool, whom she had herself seduced, was too much for her womanly vanity. All thought of love and redemption disappeared from her mind, and she gave way to a violent rage of vindictive jealousy. In a confused frenzy of anger and desire she alternately intimidated and coaxed, hardly knowing what she was doing. She revealed to Parsifal that Amfortas had been wounded by the Lance, and threatened him with a like fate. Then in feeble vacillation she put out her arms to embrace him, but he thrust her violently away, shouting, "Away, unholy woman!" In a wild paroxysm of rage she shrieked towards the castle for help, and ordered the ways to be guarded. Then, turning to Parsifal, she told him that never should he find the road he sought, for every path which took him from her she solemnly cursed, and called down upon his head the wandering malediction of her condemned days.

### The Overthrow of Klingsor's Enchanted Castle.

At the same moment Klingsor himself appeared upon the terrace of the castle carrying the sacred Lance which he hurled at Parsifal. The weapon flew towards him and stopped quivering in the air over his head. The hero raised his right hand and grasping the holy symbol made with it the sacred sign of the cross, saying :—" With this sign I exorcise thy magic; as I trust that this shall close the wound which thou hast inflicted with it, so may it overthrow thy illusory splendour in sorrow and ruins ! "

With a loud crash of thunder, an earthquake rent the entire fabric of the enchanted castle, among the ruins of which the Magician disappeared. The grove of gaudy, tropical vegetation, was withered to a desert waste, and the ground strewn with the shrivelled flowers that fell upon the arid earth. Kundry sank down prostrate amid the wreck, and Parsifal, carrying the Lance in triumph, advanced to the ruined wall of the enclosure where he paused and turned to her saying :—" Thou knowest where thou canst find me again ! "

Kundry raised herself a little, and gazed eagerly after his retreating figure.

### The Distress of the Brotherhood of the Grail.

Many sorrowful years passed away before the tragic overthrow of Klingsor's enchanted castle and Parsifal's recovery of the Sacred Lance were heard of in the Grail's domain. During this long interval the condition of the brotherhood passed from bad to worse. Not only was no remedy found for the wound of Amfortas, but he himself gradually sank into hopeless despair, craving for the release of death. To compass this selfish ambition he kept the Holy Grail imprisoned within its shrine, so that he might perish the more speedily for lack of its miraculous sustenance. The effect of this deprivation fell upon the whole brotherhood of knights, who, robbed of the potent relic, and bereft of their leader, lost all the vigour of manhood. The chivalrous enterprises of their earlier days were abandoned, since none claimed their protection, and they now wandered aimlessly about, pale and dejected. The aged king Titurel gradually pined away, and his faithful armourer, Gurnemanz, adopted the life of a hermit, and secluded himself in a remote part of the domain of the Grail. But the divine prophecy of restoration had never been withdrawn, and at length the day of deliverance dawned upon the community in Monsalvat.

## The Day of Redemption.

It was daybreak on the morning of Good Friday, and the first rays of dawn fell through the still, clear air, upon field and forest in the Grail's domain. The meadows gleamed with "vernal rapture," as if awakening to the new life of spring. In a little hut, shaded by lofty trees on the edge of the forest, the aged hermit Gurnemanz had entered upon a day of unusual sorrow. The pious hero, King Titurel, had just passed away, and with him had departed all the ancient glory of the brotherhood of the Grail. The grief of Gurnemanz was embittered by the reflection that this heavy loss was caused by the sin of Amfortas that had led to the suppression of the Holy Grail, upon which the old monarch's enfeebled frame depended for supernatural nourishment. And now, with a like fate before him, nothing remained for the old hermit but to make a pious preparation in this secluded cell, and follow his master.

Amfortas, terrified at this additional burden to his guilt, had summoned Gurnemanz and the whole community of knights to assist that day at his father's funeral, and had promised, by way of expiation, to fulfil his office and unveil the Grail.

### The Awakening of Kundry.

With these sad thoughts in his mind Gurnemanz was suddenly startled by the sound of a piteous moaning. He went to the door of his hut and listened. Again it came quite distinctly from the thicket close by, and there seemed something familiar to him in the cry. He crossed over to the bushes opposite, pulled the entwined branches apart, and there, buried in the matted tangle of overgrown thorns lay Kundry. "Up! Kundry!" he called to her, "Up! the winter has fled, and the spring is here! Awake! Awake to the spring!" He then dragged forth her rigid and lifeless form from the thicket, and bore her to a grassy mound, where he chafed her hands and brow. After a while life began to return. She awoke, opened her eyes, and then uttered a piercing cry. For a moment she stared dreamily at Gurnemanz, then rose, smoothed her hair and dress, and at once assumed the demeanour and office of a serving maid. The hermit noticed with astonishment the change in her mien and bearing. Her dress was the same coarse brown penitential robe, in which he had always seen her, but it was no longer looped up for wild riding. Her loins were no longer girt round with snakeskins, and her restless furtive glance had been replaced by a look of lowly sympathetic solicitude. When she moved as if to go about her work, the hermit reminded her that she had given him no thanks, though this was not the first time that he had roused her from deathly slumber. She only bowed her head, and muttered in hoarse and broken accents her desire to serve. He told her that her work would be light, seeing that the brotherhood sent out no messengers now and sought their own herbs ; but she paid no heed, and seeing the hut before her, forthwith entered. As Gurnemanz gazed after her with wonder there came into his benignant heart an explanation of the mysterious change which had come over her. It was the virtue of the blessed morning, the sovereign omnipotence of Good Friday, which had exorcised this victim of witchcraft, and raised her from death to life.

## The Return of Parsifal.

Now when Kundry came forth from the hut, she carried with her a pitcher and went to the spring. And looking from thence over the flowering meadows to the forest, she saw in the distance a man coming towards the woodland retreat, and she turned to Gurnemanz that she might attract his attention. The hermit gazed at the approaching figure, wondering who it could be that came to them in the gloomy gear of battle. As the stranger drew near, Kundry took her pitcher into the hut and began her work.

And now there strode out of the forest glade, with slow and solemn step, a knight, clad from head to foot in black chain-mail armour, with helmet closed, his head drooping dreamily forward, and bearing in his right hand a lowered lance. He wandered wearily towards the grassy knoll, and seated himself by the side of the spring. Gurnemanz, after gazing at him for a while in astonishment, advanced towards the traveller enquiring if he had lost his way, and whether he should direct him. But the knight only shook his head. He then asked if the mysterious visitor had no greeting for *him*. The knight again bowed his head. Annoyed at this apparent indifference, and ignorant of the knight's identity, the hermit told him that he stood upon hallowed ground, to which no man should approach in battle array, especially on such a day. "Do you know" asked Gurnemanz, "what holy day this is?" The knight once more shook his head, and the hermit told him he must indeed have come from heathen darkness not to know that this was the all-hallowed Good Friday. At this news the knight's head drooped lower still upon his breast, and when the hermit bade him take off his armour, and grieve not the Lord Who on that day, unarmed and defenceless, shed His Blood to save mankind, he rose, thrust his Lance upright in the ground, laid shield, spear, sword and helmet beside it, and knelt before it in silent prayer.

## Gurnemanz recognises Parsifal and the Sacred Lance.

And now that his helm no longer concealed the face of the knight, which was raised in loving veneration towards the point of the Lance, Gurnemanz recognised with astonishment and suppressed emotion the features of Parsifal. He beckoned to Kundry who had emerged from the hut, and told her that he identified in their mysterious visitor the youth who long ago had killed the swan. Kundry gazed intently upon the countenance of Parsifal, now altered by age and worn by strife and fatigue, and nodded her assent. Then, discerning the holy Lance, Gurnemanz blessed the happy sacred day of restoration to which he had awakened. And Parsifal, having risen from prayer and looked calmly round, recognised the hermit and gave him his hand in greeting; but Kundry turned her face away.

## Parsifal tells the Story of his Wanderings.

Gurnemanz then enquired of Parsifal from whence he came, and how. But Parsifal could hardly bring himself to tell his story. So long had he struggled, and so much had he suffered from error and opposition, that he found it difficult to believe himself at rest. He heard once more the whispering murmur of the Grail forest, he saw before him the benignant knight who had greeted him kindly in years gone by, but since those days he had unlearnt many illusions, and met with little encouragement. Incessant struggle had weakened his confidence in external things. Even there in the Grail's domain, everything seemed to him changed; so different were the dawning impressions of the innocent boy to the matured perceptions of the tried and experienced man. When the hermit asked him to whom he sought the path, Parsifal declared Amfortas to be the goal of his wanderings and the object of his mission; the wounded Amfortas whose wail had pierced his soul even in the days of his folly. Then all the misery of his wandering strife came back into his mind, and he recounted to the hermit how, driven by a curse, he had drifted perpetually from the path he thought he knew so well, ever baffled by constant struggle of conflict, disaster and despair. And all along he bore, close to his side, the holy Lance, the token of that Redeeming Love which forbade him to wield it in his own defence. To shield the sacred relic he endured many a wound, but now he brought it home again, unblemished and unstained, the gleaming Lance of the Grail!

Transported with joy the old hermit greeted the cherished relic with reverent devotion, and assured its harassed guardian that he really stood within the homestead of the Grail. He then revealed to the hero the sufferings of the Grail brotherhood, their need of deliverance, the despair of Amfortas, and the death of King Titurel. In an agony of grief at this terrible news, Parsifal flung up his arms in a torment of despair, and heaped reproaches on his own head, He it was who had caused all this misery, he who had been chosen to deliver others! What blindness, what guilt must he have incurred, that no atoning deed could deliver him from wandering error! It seemed to him then as if all his labour had been in vain, and utterly overcome with sorrow and despair, he reeled and tottered as if about to fall into a swoon. Gurnemanz advanced towards him and gently supported him to the grassy mound by the side of the holy spring.

### Kundry washes Parsifal's Feet.

And Kundry, hearing Parsifal's loud exclamation, came forth from the hut, and brought water to revive him, but Gurnemanz gently beckoned her away, choosing rather the holy well of the hermitage, since the hero had that day to be consecrated to a sacred and mystic office. And Parsifal being refreshed by the sacred spring was assisted by Gurnemanz and Kundry into a reclining posture upon the grassy knoll, and released from the armour in which he had been so long arrayed. Then he demanded of the hermit whether he would that day be conducted to Amfortas, and Gurnemanz assured him that this ambition would be satisfied as he was himself commanded to assist at the obsequies of his old master King Titurel. And now the wearied hero, clad in a tunic of white samite, reclined tranquilly upon the knoll, the aged hermit standing over him by his side, and the repentant woman kneeling at his feet, which she bathed with humble solicitude. Parsifal gazed at her for a while in silent wonder, and then he said "You have washed my feet, now let my friend besprinkle my head." And Gurnemanz, taking water from the holy well with his hand, poured it over Parsifal's head, and blessed him, saying: "Blessed be thou, pure one, through pure water! So may the sorrow of all sin depart from thee!"

### Parsifal is anointed King of the Brotherhood of the Holy Grail.

And as Gurnemanz was blessing Parsifal with the holy water, Kundry took from her bosom a golden flask, and poured ointment from it upon his feet, and having unbound her hair, dried them with her loosened tresses. Then Parsifal, gently taking the phial from her hand, gave it to Gurnemanz, that as the faithful knight of Titurel, he might anoint him King. So the hermit poured out the ointment upon Parsifal's head and laid his holy hands upon him in blessing, and hailed the chosen hero, the stainless patient sufferer, by pity made wise unto salvation, as King of the Grail. And having done this, he entreated Parsifal once more to extend his compassion to Amfortas, whose sorrows he had shared, and take the last burden from the head of the wounded sufferer.

### Parsifal Baptises Kundry.

But Parsifal bent down unperceived, and taking water in his hand from the holy spring, he poured it over Kundry's head and baptised her. His first act of princely clemency was to break the chains of that spell-bound captive, whose wandering curse he had borne so long. And when he spoke in tones of compassionate tenderness and said to her "Be baptised, and believe on the Redeemer!" she bowed her contrite head upon the earth, overwhelmed—at last—with weeping.

### The Magic of Good Friday.

Then Parsifal bent his eyes towards the flowering meadow lands, now gleaming in the golden light of morning; and rapt in gentle ecstasy, he hailed the fair enchantment of the scene. He spoke of magic flowers which once he chanced to meet that raised their heads and would have clasped him with their hungry tendrils. But never had he seen the like of those he now beheld, no grass so smooth and soft, no flowers and blossoms so fragrant with the scents recalling childhood's days, so sweetly eloquent of simple love and trust. The hermit then revealed to him that this glory was the magic of Good Friday. And Parsifal asked whether every living thing should not rather mourn and sorrow on such a day of agony. But the hermit answered that the glow of beauty upon the fields and flowers of the Grail was given by the tears of contrite sinners, which fell like holy dew upon the earth. Moreover, on that day of redemption the whole creation flushed with joy at the gleaming trace of the Redeemer, and yearned to consecrate its prayers to Him in bounden duty. For though it had no power to see Him on the Cross, yet still it looked up confident to man redeemed. It looked up to humanity, liberated and cleansed through God's Sacrifice of Love, and trusted that since with infinite patience and boundless compassion God had suffered for man, so would the ransomed human race walk gently now on blade and blossom. Thus did the fading herbs and withering flowers, which linger for a little while and then go hence, bide their appointed time with gratitude, since nature purified had won her day of innocence. And when the hermit had finished speaking, Kundry slowly raised her head once more, and through the tears that filled her eyes, gazed with a calm, earnest, beseeching look towards Parsifal. And he, regarding her with tender pity, spoke of the flowers that once had laughed to him, and then had withered, and wondered whether they also pined for redemption upon that sacred morning! He marked the holy dew of blessed contrite tears which down her cheeks were flowing. "Thou weepest," he said, "see the meadow lands are smiling!" Then bending down he gently kissed her brow.

### PARSIFAL IS AGAIN CONDUCTED TO THE HALL OF THE HOLY GRAIL.

And now through the tranquil air there came the sound of the great bells of Monsalvat calling the brotherhood to the sacred ceremony. So Gurnemanz brought out his knightly mantle, and laid it upon the shoulders of Parsifal, who grasped with solemn reverence the sacred Lance, and, accompanied by Kundry, went forth to follow the aged hermit.

### The Healing of Amfortas.

Meanwhile, within the sacred fortress, all were preparing for the solemn ceremony. Through the great doors leading into the hall of the Holy Grail marched two processions of knights, one carrying the body of King Titurel, and the other the wounded Amfortas, preceded by the shrine of the sacred relic. As these solemn processions advanced into the vast refectory, they declaimed to each other antiphonally the tragedies associated with their respective burdens.

And when Amfortas had been set down on the litter behind the raised table of the Grail, the knights called upon him to fulfil his office, and once more, for the last time, unveil the Holy Cup. But he, having raised himself painfully from his couch, gazed before him upon his father's corpse, and burst into a wild lamentation of sorrow and remorse, calling upon his brother knights to release him from the torture and burden of his miserable existence. In a passionate appeal to the venerated hero that lay dead before him, whose eyes were bent in rapture on the face of Christ, he implored his intercession that the life-giving glory of the Holy Grail should be poured out upon the brotherhood, but that to him might be granted restoration and release in the eternal rest of death.

Impatient at his halting cowardice the knights now crowded angrily around Amfortas, and in loud clamour demanded the exposition of the sacred token. Springing to his feet the wounded king rushed down the steps into the midst of the startled community, and tearing open the garment which concealed his bleeding wound, begged them to plunge their swords deep into his heart. As the knights shrank back affrighted at the terrible aspect of their frenzied leader, Parsifal, who had entered the Hall unobserved with Gurnemanz and Kundry, advanced towards Amfortas, touched him with the sacred weapon that once had cleft his side, and closed the wound for ever. In that moment the tide of yearning was stemmed, the torrent of sinful desire turned back, and the surge of human passion laid to rest. The countenance of the healed monarch became radiant with celestial rapture, and overcome with deep emotion he staggered towards Gurnemanz for support.

### Parsifal Unveils the Holy Grail and Kundry Dies.

Then Parsifal advancing to the centre of the knights, raised aloft the sacred Lance, and called upon the brotherhood to welcome back the holy weapon. As they gazed upwards in rapture, Parsifal, turning towards the point of the Lance, burst into an inspired declamation in praise of the miraculous relic, and all beheld that it gleamed crimson with the Tide of Love, which yearned to join the taintless fountain in the Grail. "No more," he cried, "shall it be veiled. Unveil the Grail! Open the shrine!" He ascended the steps whilst the youths removed the cover of the reliquary, and brought forth the crystal Chalice, before which he then knelt in silent prayer. The daylight waned, the air vibrated with mysterious music, the glowing Chalice of Redeeming Love burned like a beacon on the holy hill, the knights below and choir upon choir in the heights of the dome took up the strain :—

> " Marvel of highest Redemption !
> Redemption to the Redeemer ! "

In a resplendent ray of purest light, which fell from the dome, there hovered over the head of Parsifal a white dove. Kundry, who had slowly pressed her weary feet after her deliverer, now fell upon her knees and raised her eyes to Parsifal. Then she sank slowly to the ground and died, ransomed and transfigured, the brightest refulgence of the Grail's redeeming glory falling upon her upraised face. Gurnemanz and Amfortas, with the whole brotherhood of the Grail, knelt in veneration, whilst Parsifal waved the glowing symbol of Christ's redeeming Love in benediction over all mankind. For the ransomed of the Lord had returned and come to Zion, with songs, and everlasting joy upon their heads, and sorrow, and sighing, had fled away.

---

# THE MUSICAL DRAMA.

[NOTE.—*The Editors have attempted to give here a plain literal prose translation of the text of the Drama, together with a few explanatory notes of their own which are always printed in italics, and enclosed in brackets. The bracketed numerals dispersed throughout the text indicate the numbers attached to the musical themes commencing on page* 112.]

# PARSIFAL:

## *A SACRED FESTIVAL-DRAMA*

BY

RICHARD WAGNER.

---

*CHARACTERS.*

| | |
|---|---|
| AMFORTAS. | PARSIFAL. |
| TITUREL. | KLINGSOR. |
| GURNEMANZ. | KUNDRY. |

Knights of the Grail and Esquires. Klingsor's Magic Maidens.

---

PLACE OF ACTION:—In the domain of the Grail, and in the Castle of the Grail-keepers, "Monsalvat." Landscape characteristic of the northern mountains of Gothic Spain. Afterwards, Klingsor's Magic Castle on the southern slopes of the same mountains, which must be supposed to face Arabian Spain. The dress of the Knights of the Grail and of the Esquires resembles that of the Knights Templars, white tabards and mantles; but instead of the red cross a hovering Dove embroidered on the escutcheons and the mantles.

[*The tabards now worn are pale blue, and the mantles scarlet.*]

*[The reader must imagine himself to be seated in the theatre at Bayreuth. The building is darkened and silent; the orchestra concealed in a sunken space between the auditorium and the stage, so that the hearer is brought into undisturbed contact with the mystery-drama and its music.]*

* * * * * *

# ACT I.

---

## THE PRELUDE.

*[The Prelude begins, the opening theme emerging softly in single low tones out of the stillness. It is the theme of divine self-oblation, sung afterwards to the words "Take unto you My Body, take unto you My Blood; the symbol of our love."* [1a.] *A quivering wave-like movement now rises from the orchestra, and soaring upwards carries the melody as if on wings, until it seems "to go right up to heaven and die among the stars." There is silence for a moment, and then in single low tones the second phrase of the same theme softly rises, and*

*is borne aloft as before.* [1b.] *The first note of the sacred mystery has been given, the keynote of the drama of divine love, such as brought God down from heaven to earth. It is fitly followed by a theme always associated with the Holy Grail, the glowing symbol of Christ's ardent pity.* [4.] *These themes of Love's Sacrifice and its symbol give place to a grand hymn of faith, at first proclaimed aloud on trumpets, and afterwards begun softly, and then gradually broadened to a majestic cadence, gathering strength as it descends from step to step.* [5.]

*Thus do these themes of compassionate love and chivalrous faith announce the active spiritual principles of the drama, but the love which redeems through pity, and the faith which works through love, are only made perfect by suffering. Therefore when the theme of the divine self-oblation wells up once more in single notes, it rises from a roll of ominous murmuring, and out of it are here emphasized two phrases, one associated with suffering* [2], *and the other with the sacred Lance.* [3.] *The first is sobbed out again and again, and seems to hinder and traverse the main theme as it is carried upward from key to key. It is then supplanted by the piercing Lance phrase, that is lifted higher and higher until it culminates in an outburst of passionate grief upon the theme which utters the Wail of God for the sin of fallen man* [16], *and then sinks down and sighs itself away. Then comes the end. The tragedy of sin and suffering is foreshadowed, but over all, and at the end of all, is "The Heart of the Eternal Which is most wonderfully kind." The Son of God is ever crucified afresh, yet ever offers Himself. Once more the opening notes of the divine self-oblation theme soar upwards, and are carried aloft till we lose them at the feet of God: "Take unto you My Body, take unto you My Blood; the symbol of our Love."*]

---

[*The following description of the Prelude, written by Richard Wagner himself as a kind of explanatory programme, is reprinted here from the "Meister" (No. II.), by the kind permission of its translator, Mr. W. Ashton Ellis.*]

# "LOVE—FAITH—HOPE!"

---

## First Theme: "LOVE."

"Take ye My Body, take My Blood, in token of our Love!"

(Repeated in whispers, ever fainter, by angel-voices.)

"Take ye My Blood, My Body take, and think of Me."

(Again whisperingly repeated.)

## Second Theme: "FAITH."

Promise of Redemption through Faith. Strong and firm does Faith reveal itself, lofty and resolute even in suffering. In answer to the renewed promise, sounds soft the voice of Faith from dimmest heights —as though borne on the wings of the snow-white Dove — slowly descending — embracing with ever greater breadth and fulness, the heart of man, filling the world and the whole of nature with mightiest force; then—as though stilled to rest—glancing upwards again toward the light of heaven. Once more from the awe of solitude arises the lament of loving compassion, the agony, the Holy Sweat of the Mount of Olives, the divine sufferings of Golgotha —the Body blanches, the Blood streams forth and glows in the chalice with the heavenly glow of blessing, pouring forth on all that lives and languishes the gracious gift of Redemption through Love. For him are we prepared, for Amfortas, the sinful guardian of the shrine, who—with heart gnawed by fearful rue for sin—must prostrate himself before the chastisement of the vision of the Grail. Shall there be redemption from the devouring torments of his soul? Yet once again we hear the promise, and—hope.

---

# ACT I.

SCENE.—In the domain of the Grail. Forest, shady and solemn, but not gloomy. A glade in the centre. Rising to the left the supposed way to the Castle of the Grail. Towards the centre of the background the landscape sinks down to a forest lake lying somewhat lower.—Daybreak.—Gurnemanz (old but vigorous) and two Esquires (tender youths) are lying asleep under a tree.—From the left side, as if from the Castle of the Grail, comes the sound of the solemn reveille on trombones. [1.]

GURNEMANZ.

(Awaking and shaking the Esquires.)

Hey! Ho! Guardians of the forest, or rather guardians of sleep, at least awake to the morning. [4.]

(The two Esquires spring up.)

You hear the call? Thank God that you are called to hear it.

(He sinks on to his knees with the Esquires, and joins with them in silently offering up the morning prayer. [5.]

(They rise slowly.) [4.]

Now up, my lads! [5.] See to the bath. It is time to wait upon the King there. [6.] Already I can see the runners who go before his litter.

(Two Knights enter, coming from the Castle.)

Hail to you! How fares Amfortas to-day? He has asked for his bath very early: I hope and trust the healing herb which Gawaine used such skill and daring to secure, has given him relief?

SECOND KNIGHT.

Can you hope that, you who know all? The pain soon came back with even greater intensity: sleepless from strong paroxysms of pain, he begged eagerly for his bath.

GURNEMANZ.

(Sadly bowing his head.)

Fools we, to hope for relief, when a thorough cure alone avails! [7.] We may search for every herb and potion throughout the wide world, but only one availeth, only the ONE. [7.]

SECOND KNIGHT.

Then tell us who that is!

GURNEMANZ.

(Evasively.)

Attend to the bath!

SECOND ESQUIRE.

(Turning towards the background with First Esquire, and looking to the right.)

See there the wild woman riding!

FIRST ESQUIRE.

Hey! Look at the flowing mane of the devil's mare!

SECOND KNIGHT.

Ha! Is it Kundry?

FIRST KNIGHT.

Surely she brings urgent tidings?

SECOND ESQUIRE.

The mare staggers. [8a.]

FIRST ESQUIRE.

Has she flown through the air?

SECOND ESQUIRE.

Now she crawls on the ground.

FIRST ESQUIRE.

She brushes the moss with her mane.

(All look off eagerly towards the Right.)

SECOND ESQUIRE.

There, the wild witch is swinging herself off.

(Kundry rushes in hastily, almost staggering. Wild dress, looped up high; girdle of snakeskins hanging down long; black hair flowing in loose locks; dark reddish brown complexion; piercing black eyes, at times flashing wildly, more often expressionless and fixed as in death. She hastens to Gurnemanz and presses a small crystal flask on him.) [**8b.**]

KUNDRY.

Here! Take it! Balsam! [**8c.**]

GURNEMANZ.

From whence did you bring this?

KUNDRY.

From further than you can imagine. [**8c.**] If this balsam fails, naught else in Arabia will avail. Ask no further. I am weary.

(She flings herself on the ground.)

(A train of Esquires and Knights enter from the Left, bearing and attending the litter on which Amfortas lies outstretched. Gurnemanz turns from Kundry to the new comers.) [**6.**]

GURNEMANZ.

He comes, borne on a litter. Alas! how can I bear to see the Lord of the most glorious race [**9**] in the proud bloom of his manhood, the slave of sickness? [2.]

(To the Esquires.)

Be careful! Hark! The King is groaning.

(The Esquires stop and set down the litter.)

AMFORTAS.

(Raising himself a little.)

That is well!—I thank you! Rest awhile.—After a wild night of agony [6] behold the morning splendour of the forest! [10a.] The water of the holy lake will likewise refresh me. The pain is numbed, the dark night of agony melts into the light of day. Gawaine—

SECOND KNIGHT.

Sire! Gawaine did not stay: as soon as he knew that the herb which he had procured with such difficulty betrayed your hopes, he hastened forth on a new quest.

AMFORTAS.

Without permission!—May he make amends for thus disregarding the laws of the Grail Knighthood! Oh woe to him, however brave he be, if he falls into Klingsor's snares! Let none of you ever give me cause for a like anxiety! I wait for him who is decreed me:—"By pity enlightened"—were not those the words? [7.]

GURNEMANZ.

That is what you said they were.

AMFORTAS.

"The stainless fool," I think I should recognise him if I might style him "DEATH."

GURNEMANZ.

(Handing Kundry's flask to Amfortas.)

But yet, give this balsam a trial!

AMFORTAS.

(Contemplating it.)

Where did this mysterious flask come from? [8c.]

GURNEMANZ.

It was brought to you from Arabia.

AMFORTAS.

And who procured it?

GURNEMANZ.

The wild woman who lies yonder. Up, Kundry! Come! [8a and b.]

(Kundry refuses and remains on the ground.)

AMFORTAS.

*You*, Kundry? Have I to thank you again, you scared and restless woman? [8b.] Well, then, I will yet give this balsam a trial, out of gratitude for your kindness.

KUNDRY.

(Moving restlessly and impetuously on the ground.)

Do not thank me! Ha, ha!—What good can it do? [8b.] Give me no thanks! Away, away to thy bath!

(Amfortas gives the signal to go on; the procession retires

towards the back.—Gurnemanz gazing after them sadly, and Kundry still lying on the ground, remain behind. Esquires come and go.) [6.] [10a.]

THIRD ESQUIRE.

Hey! You there! Why do you lie crouching like a wild beast?

KUNDRY.

Are not the wild beasts sacred here? [4.]

THIRD ESQUIRE.

Yes, but we do not feel certain that *you* are sacred.

FOURTH ESQUIRE.

I believe she will utterly destroy our Master with her magic drugs. [8b.]

GURNEMANZ.

H'm! What harm has she ever done *you*? When we have all been perplexed how to communicate with our brethren fighting in distant lands, hardly knowing where they were, has not *she* been the watchful messenger, who before we have come to our senses has rushed off and returned, fulfilling her mission with good fortune and fidelity? She is beholden to you for neither food, nor home, nor does she share anything in common with you; but when it is a question of help in time of danger, her zeal transports her through the air, and yet she never looks to you for thanks. You may call this injury, but to my mind it is good service.

THIRD ESQUIRE.

But she hates us—only look how malevolently she glares at us!

FOURTH ESQUIRE.

She is a Pagan, [8a] and a sorceress. [8b.]

GURNEMANZ.

Yes, she may be bewitched. She lives here now, perhaps regenerated, that she may expiate [1] the unforgiven sins of a former life. [8b.] And if she does penance through good works, which benefit our Grail Knighthood [7] she does right well [5], for assuredly she serves us and likewise helps herself.

THIRD ESQUIRE.

Perchance it is through her guilt that so much distress has come upon us?

GURNEMANZ.

(Reflecting.)

Yes, whenever she has been absent for a long time, trouble has come. I have known her long, but Titurel still longer. When he built yon castle, he found her asleep in the thicket here, rigid and lifeless, as if dead. And so I found her myself lately, just after the misfortune happened which that wicked one across the mountains so ignominiously brought upon us. [11.] Hey! you! Listen and speak: where were you wandering about [8b] when our monarch lost the Lance?

(Kundry keeps gloomily silent.) [11.]

Why did you not help us then?

KUNDRY.

I never help.

FOURTH ESQUIRE.

She says so herself.

THIRD ESQUIRE.

If she is so loyal, so brave in our defence, send her to recover the lost Lance!

GURNEMANZ.

Ah! That is another matter. That is forbidden to all. [2.]

(With great emotion.)

O wondrous Lance, [3] emblazoned with the Precious Blood! I saw thee brandished by most sacrilegious hand!

(Lost in recollection.)

[2] [3.] When armed with thee what could hinder the dauntless Amfortas from vanquishing the magician? [9.] Close beneath the fortress the young monarch was separated from us: a woman of appalling beauty had bewitched him, in her arms he lay entranced: [11] the Lance dropped from his hand; [2] [3] a cry of deathly agony! [8b.] I rushed towards him: Klingsor vanished laughing, [11] he had carried off the sacred Lance. [3.] I fought to cover the king's retreat; but a wound was burning in his side, [2] the wound that will not heal. [3.]

(The First and Second Esquires return from the lake.) [6.]

THIRD ESQUIRE.

Then you knew Klingsor?

GURNEMANZ.

(To the two returning Esquires.)

How fares the King?

FIRST ESQUIRE.

He is refreshed by his bath. [10a.]

SECOND ESQUIRE.

The balsam has eased the pain.

GURNEMANZ.

(Aside)

It is the wound which never can be closed! [6.]

THIRD ESQUIRE.

But father, tell us, you knew Klingsor? How was that?

(The Third and Fourth Esquires had already seated themselves at Gurnemanz's feet, the two others now join them, under the big tree.)

GURNEMANZ.

The pious hero Titurel knew him well. For when the domain of the true faith was threatened by the craft and power of Pagan barbarians, there came down in the midst of holy night, [13] sacred messengers of the Lord Jesus [4] who gave into our hero's care that precious vessel, [4] the hallowed noble cup, from which the Lord Himself drank at His last Feast of Love, [1] and into which His Godly Blood flowed when He hung upon the cross: [25] also the Lance which shed that Blood, [3]—these testimonies of highest miracles of beneficence, they gave into our King's keeping. [13.] For this holy treasure Titurel built a sanctuary, [4] you who have been called to its service by paths concealed from sinners, know that none but the pure are allowed to join this brotherhood, to which the miraculous power of the Grail gives strength to excel in saving works of deliverance. [4.] Wherefore this Klingsor of whom ye ask was denied admission, hard as he strove to gain it. He lived as a hermit over in yon valley, beyond which lies the openest heathendom: [12] I never discovered what sin he had committed there, [11] but he was ready to repent, nay even to become holy. Powerless to kill sin in his soul, he laid a guilty hand upon his body, and this hand he again stretched forth towards the Grail. Its guardian spurned him scornfully. At this he was enraged, and his fury disclosed to him that his infamous act could give him counsel in the use of wicked magic; which he now turned to account. [11.] [8b.] He transformed the desert into a wondrous garden of delight [18] peopled with women of diabolical beauty; and there he lies in wait to lure the Knights of the Grail to the pleasures of sin and the pains of hell; [8b] those who are entrapped fall into his power, and many there are who have met this fate. [8b.] Now when King Titurel grew very old he conferred the lordship upon his son [4] Amfortas, who spared no effort to end this magic scourge. You know what happened afterwards, the Lance [3] is now in Klingsor's hands, [11] and if he can use it to wound even our holy knights, he will doubtless begin to believe that the Grail itself is within his grasp! [12.]

(Kundry has often turned herself violently round in agonised disquietude.)

FOURTH ESQUIRE.

The first thing to be done then is to recover the Lance!

THIRD ESQUIRE.

Ah! He who did that would gain glory and good fortune!

GURNEMANZ.

Prostrate before the plundered sanctuary [4] in impassioned prayer, Amfortas piteously implored for a token of redemption: [2] whereupon a holy radiance floated from the Grail, [4] and there shone forth the vision of One [1] Who spoke these words:—

By pity enlightened,
The stainless Fool:
Wait for him,
My chosen One. [7.]

THE FOUR ESQUIRES.
(Together.)

By pity enlightened,
The stainless Fool. [7.]

(From the lake are heard the shouts and cries of Knights and Esquires. Gurnemanz and the four Esquires start up and turn round in alarm.) [14.]

KNIGHTS AND ESQUIRES.

Alas! Alas! Hoho! Up! Who is the culprit?

(A wild swan flutters feebly from the lake; the Esquires and Knights follow after it on to the stage.)

GURNEMANZ.

What is the matter?

FOURTH ESQUIRE.

There!

THIRD ESQUIRE.

Here!

SECOND ESQUIRE.

A swan!

FOURTH ESQUIRE.

A wild swan!

THIRD ESQUIRE.

It is wounded!

KNIGHTS AND ESQUIRES.

Ha! Alas! Alas!

GURNEMANZ.

Who shot the swan?

(The swan, after a painful flight falls helplessly to the ground the Second Knight draws the arrow out of its breast.)

FIRST KNIGHT.

The swan was circling around the lake and the king greeted it as a good omen, [10b] when an arrow flew—

OTHER KNIGHTS AND ESQUIRES.

(Bringing in Parsifal.)

T'was he! He shot it! There is the bow!

SECOND KNIGHT.

Here is the arrow just like his.

GURNEMANZ.

(To Parsifal.)

Is it you who killed this swan?

PARSIFAL.

To be sure! I shoot every flying thing! [14.]

GURNEMANZ.

Did you do this? And are you not aghast at what you have done?

KNIGHTS AND ESQUIRES.

Punish the culprit!

GURNEMANZ.

Inconceivable act! You could do murder? *Here* amidst the peaceful stillness of the holy forest? Did not the living creatures of the woodland approach you without fear, and was not their welcome friendly and confiding? What did the little birds sing to you from the branches of the trees? [10a.] What harm had the faithful swan done to you? He was soaring aloft to find his mate and sail with her around the lake, [10b] conferring thus a glorious consecration [4] on the healing bath. Were you not filled with wonder? Did it only tempt you to a reckless boyish bowshot? [14. 3.] To us he was dear: what is he now to you? [3.] Here, see! Here you struck him; there the blood is not yet cold,—the wings hang helpless; the snowy plumage is darkly stained,—his eye is dimmed,—do you see its look?

(Parsifal who has listened with increasing emotion to Gurnemanz now breaks his bow in pieces, and flings away his arrows.) [14. 3.]

Are you conscious of your sin?

(Parsifal draws his hand across his eyes.) [3.]

Say, my lad, do you realize the depth of your guilt? [2.] How could you incur it?

PARSIFAL.

I did not know it.

GURNEMANZ.

Where do you come from? [14.]

PARSIFAL.

I do not know.

GURNEMANZ.

Who is your father?

PARSIFAL.

I do not know. [2.]

GURNEMANZ.

Who sent you here?

PARSIFAL.

I do not know.

GURNEMANZ.

Your name then?

PARSIFAL.

I once had many, but now I remember none of them. [20a.]

GURNEMANZ.

You know nothing of all this? [14].

(Aside.)

This is the dullest dolt I have ever met with save Kundry!

(To the Esquires who have collected in larger numbers.)

Now go! Do not neglect the King in his bath! [6.] Lend a hand!

(The Esquires lift the dead swan reverently on to a bier of green branches, and retire with it towards the lake. [10b.] Finally only Gurnemanz, Parsifal and (apart) Kundry, remain behind.)

GURNEMANZ.

(Turning again to Parsifal.)

Now say! You know nothing of what I have asked you, but speak and tell me what you *do* know, for surely you must know something.

PARSIFAL.

I have a mother; her name is Herzeleide. [**20a.**] Our home was in the forest and wild moorlands. [**14.**]

GURNEMANZ.

Who gave you your bow?

PARSIFAL.

I made it for myself, to drive the wild eagles from the forest. [**14.**]

GURNEMANZ.

But you seem to be noble and well-born, why then did not your mother have you trained to better weapons?

KUNDRY.

(Kundry, during Gurnemanz's description of the fall of Amfortas, has many times violently turned herself round in agitated disquietude. And now, still crouching in the corner of the wood, she keeps her eyes fixed upon Parsifal, and seeing that he remains silent, calls out with a harsh voice.)

He was fatherless when his mother bore him, [**20a**] for Gamuret was slain in battle; to shield her son from a like heroic early death she reared him in the desert as a fool and ignorant of arms, [7] the foolish woman!

(She laughs.) [8b.]

PARSIFAL.

(Who has listened intently.)

Yes! And once there came along the verge of the forest glittering men seated on beautiful animals; I wished to be like them: they laughed and galloped away. [8a.] I followed but I could not overtake them; [14.] I passed through deserts, up hill and down dale; often it was night, then day again: I had to use my bow against wild beasts and great men. [8a.]

KUNDRY.

(Who has risen and joined the group.)

(Eagerly.)

Yes! Ruffians and giants felt his strength; they learnt to fear the fierce boy. [8a 14.]

PARSIFAL.

(Surprised.)

Who fears me? Say!

KUNDRY.

The wicked.

PARSIFAL.

Were those who threatened me wicked? [8a.]

(Gurnemanz laughs.)

Who is good?

GURNEMANZ.

(Again serious.)

Your mother, whom you deserted, and who grieves and laments for you. [20 a.]

KUNDRY.

She grieves no more; [8a.] his mother is dead. [8b.]

PARSIFAL.

(In terrible fear.)

Dead?—My mother?—Who says so?

KUNDRY.

I rode by and saw her die: [8a.] to thee, fool, she sent her greeting by me.

(Parsifal springs furiously upon Kundry and seizes her by the throat.) [14.]

GURNEMANZ.

(Holding Parsifal back.)

You mad boy! Violence again?

(After Gurnemanz has released Kundry, Parsifal stands dazed for a while.) [20a.]

What harm has the woman done to you? She spoke the truth; for Kundry never lies, though she has seen much.

PARSIFAL.

(Beginning to tremble violently.)

I am fainting!

(Kundry perceiving Parsifal's condition hastens to a forest spring and brings water in a horn. She first sprinkles Parsifal with it, and then gives him to drink.) [8a.]

GURNEMANZ.

That is well! For so according to the grace of the Grail: he banishes evil who gives good in return for it. [8c.]

KUNDRY.

(Gloomily.)

I never do good.

(She turns away sadly, and while Gurnemanz attends Parsifal with fatherly care, she drags herself unnoticed towards a thicket.)

It is only rest I long for, only rest ; [11.] ah ! What weariness. Sleep! Oh, let none awake me !

(Starting in terror. [8b.]

No ! Not sleep ! Terror seizes me ! [12.]

(Trembling violently, and letting her arms hang helpless.)

Vain to resist ! The time has come. Sleep—sleep : *I must !* [11.]

(She sinks down behind the thicket, and is seen no more. Some movement is perceived near the lake, and eventually the train of Knights and Esquires pass at back carrying the litter homeward.)

GURNEMANZ.

The King is returning from his bath ; [15b] the sun is high in the heaven : now let me conduct you to the Holy Feast, and if you are pure, the Grail will be both meat and drink to you.

(Gurnemanz has laid Parsifal's arm tenderly round his own neck, and clasped the boy's body with his arm ; in this way he leads him along with slow steps.) [15b.]

PARSIFAL.

Who is the Grail ? [4.]

GURNEMANZ.

That may not be told ; but, if you are chosen to serve it, this knowledge will not be concealed from you. And see ! I think I have recognised you aright ! The pathway to the Grail leads not through the land, nor could anyone find it save he whom the Grail itself directs. [15b.]

PARSIFAL.

I hardly step, and yet I seem already far.

GURNEMANZ.

You see, my son, that time here becomes space.

(While Gurnemanz and Parsifal have appeared to walk, the scene has been gradually moving from Left to Right; in this manner the forest disappears, and a causeway in rocky walls is disclosed to view, which conceals them both.)

[*The music accompanying the moving scenery, and the passing of Gurnemanz and Parsifal from the woodland glade to the hall of the Holy Grail, begins with a march suggested by the four notes rung upon the bells of the Castle of Monsalvat* [15a *and* b.] *This merges into a contrapuntal movement, possibly suggested by themes* 4 *and* 5, *which ascends with increasing force and complexity, until it culminates in a piercing wail of anguish,* [16] *repeated four times with ever-increasing agony. As we approach the hall of the Grail a loud blast of trumpets,* [1] *and the clang of deep bells* [15a] *are heard calling the knights to the Sacred Feast. Of this music Wagner himself said:—" The unrolling of the moving scene, however artistically carried out, was emphatically not intended for decorative effect alone; but, under the influence of the accompanying music, we were, as in a state of dreamy rapture, to be led imperceptibly along the trackless ways to the Castle of the Grail; by which means, at the same time, its traditional inaccessibility, for those who are not called, was drawn into the domain of dramatic performance."*

GESAMMELTE SCHRIFTEN, X. page 305, (Edition 1888.)

(Leading through ascending vaulted passages the scene has been completely changed. Gurnemanz and Parsifal now enter a mighty hall, the refectory of the Grail Brotherhood, [4] surmounted by a high vaulted dome, through which alone the daylight pours.)

GURNEMANZ.

(To Parsifal who stands like one dazed.)

Now pay attention; and if you are a fool, and pure, let me see what knowledge and wisdom may be given to you. [15b.] [4.]

(The great doors on either side at the back are opened. From the Right the Knights of the Grail march in in solemn procession, and during the singing which follows take their places round the refectory tables, [4] upon which are cups only.)

KNIGHTS.

Day by day we come prepared for the Feast of Love, [15a and b] as if it were to refresh us for the last time. To him who rejoices in good works the Feast is ever renewed: he may approach and be comforted by receiving the most holy gift.

(At this point Amfortas is carried in on a litter by Esquires and serving brothers through the opposite door; before him march four Esquires who carry the shrine of the Holy Grail, draped with a crimson cover. This train proceeds to the centre of the background, where is erected a raised couch, on to which Amfortas is set down from his litter; in front of this stands an oblong table of stone, on which the youths place the draped shrine of the Grail.)

YOUTHS' VOICES.

(From the mid-height of the dome as Amfortas is carried in.)

As once, with a thousand pains, His Blood flowed for sinful worlds, so now let my blood be joyfully shed for the Hero of Salvation. [16.] May the Body which He offered for our atonement live in us through His death. [16.]

BOYS' VOICES.

(From the extreme height of the dome.)

Faith lives; the Dove hovers, the Saviour's Holy Messenger: receive the Wine which flows for you, and partake of the Bread of Life! [5.]

(When the singing is ended and all the Knights have taken their places at the tables, a long silence ensues. From the far background is heard coming from a vaulted niche behind Amfortas' couch, as if from a grave, the voice of the aged Titurel.)

TITUREL'S VOICE.

My son Amfortas, wilt thou fulfil thine office?

(A long silence.)

Am I this day to look upon the Grail once more and live?

(A long silence.)

Must I go hence without my Saviour for my guide?

AMFORTAS.

(Half raising himself, in an outburst of agonised despair.)

Alas! Alas for my agony! [16.] My father, oh! fulfil thou once more the office! Live! Live, and let me die!

TITUREL.

Entombed I live on through my Saviour's grace, [4] though I am too weak to serve Him. Atone thy guilt by good works. Unveil ye the Grail! [4.]

AMFORTAS.

(Rising to restrain the boys.)

No! [8b.] Leave it unrevealed! Oh! May no one fathom the torture which pierces me at the vision which enraptures you! What is the wound and the fury of its pain, compared with the misery and hell torment of being condemned to this office? Woeful the inheritance which has fallen to my lot, that I, the only sinner amongst you all, must guard the highest sanctuary, and pray for its blessing to be poured out upon the pure! Oh, punishment! Chastisement beyond compare of the outraged gracious One! [16.] For Him, and for His welcome of consecration must I throb with yearning; from holy penitence within my deepest soul [16] must I approach Him. The hour draws nigh:—a ray of light descends upon the sacred rite; [4] the veil falls. [1.] The Divine Treasure in the sacred Chalice glows with radiant power; enraptured with beatific pain I feel the fountain of the most Holy One's Blood poured into my heart: [1] but the surge of my own sinful blood [6] rushes back in mad flight, and in wild terror pours itself into the world of sinful desire; [11] again it forces the floodgate from which it now streams forth, here, through the wound, like to His, struck by a blow of the same Lance, [2] that in the same place pierced the Saviour's wound, [16] from whence with tears of blood the Divine One wept with holy, longing pity, for the disgrace of mankind, [16]—and now, in this holy place, [4] from out of me, guardian of the most divine treasures, keeper of the balsam of redemption, [4] [8b] the hot blood of sin surges, [11] ever renewed from the fountain of desire, [12] which, alas! no atonement ever quenches in me! [8b.] Mercy! Mercy! Thou all-merciful One! [3] Oh! Have mercy! Take mine inheritance, close the wound, that I may die holy, pure once more in Thy sight! [3.]

(He falls back as though unconscious.)

BOYS' VOICES.

(From the dome.)

By pity enlightened,
The stainless Fool:
Wait for him,
My chosen One. [7.]

THE KNIGHTS.

(Softly.)

Thus was it decreed for thee: wait on in hope; fulfil thine office to-day! [4.]

TITUREL.

Unveil the Grail! [4.]

(Amfortas raises himself slowly and with effort. The boys unveil the golden shrine and bring forth the ancient crystal Cup which they likewise uncover, and set before Amfortas.) [2.]

VOICES FROM THE HEIGHT.

Take unto you My Body, take unto you My Blood; the symbol of our Love. [1a.]

(While Amfortas bends reverently before the chalice in silent prayer, a gradually increasing darkness fills the Hall.) [1a.]

BOYS' VOICES FROM THE HEIGHT.

Take unto you My Blood, take unto you My Body, in remembrance of Me. [1b.]

(Here a blinding ray of light falls from above upon the crystal Cup, which then glows with an increasing crimson lustre, diffusing a gentle radiance on all around [1b.] Amfortas with transfigured mien, raises the Grail on high, and waves it gently in all directions, and then blesses the bread and wine [3.] As the darkness began all had fallen on their knees, and now raise their eyes reverently to the Grail.)

### Titurel's Voice.

Oh! Celestial Rapture! how glorious to-day is the salutation of the Lord. [16.]

(Amfortas sets down the Grail which gradually ceases to glow as the daylight returns; thereupon the four boys replace the Chalice in the shrine which they veil as before [4]; they now take the two flagons and the two baskets of bread which Amfortas had blessed before by waving the Grail Chalice over them from the altar-table, divide the bread among the knights, and fill the goblets standing before them with wine. The knights sit down to the meal and so does Gurnemanz, who keeps a place vacant beside him and beckons to Parsifal to partake of the meal; but Parsifal remains standing at the side, rigid and silent, as though in a trance.)

### Antiphonal Singing During the Feast.

[*The melody employed here is suggested by Theme No.* 1.]

### Boys' Voices from the Height.

Through the power of pity and of love, the Lord of the Grail transformed the bread and wine at His Last Feast, into the Blood Which He shed, and the Body Which He offered up.

### Youths' Voices from the Mid-height.

The Body and the Blood of the divine oblation is this day transformed for your refreshment, by the loving spirit of sacred consolation, into the wine now poured out for you, and into the bread which ye now eat.

KNIGHTS (*first half*).

Take of the bread, boldly transform it into bodily strength and power; faithful till death, braving every danger, to perform the works of the Saviour.

KNIGHTS (*second half*).

Take of the wine, transform it anew into the fiery blood of life.

KNIGHTS (*all*).

Rejoicing to fight in comradeship, with holy courage, faithful as brothers.

ALL.

Blessed in Faith! Blessed in Love [4]!

YOUTHS' VOICES.

(From the mid-height.)

Blessed in Love!

BOYS' VOICES.

(From the extreme height.)

Blessed in Faith! [4]

(The knights having risen advance from both sides and embrace each other solemnly. [4.] During the meal, of which he had not partaken, Amfortas has gradually receded from his state of inspired exultation; he bows his head and presses his hand upon the wound, which has broken out afresh. The boys tend him, and assist him on to his litter, and while all are preparing to disperse, bear him away preceded by the sacred shrine. [16.] The Knights and Esquires gradually leave the hall in solemn procession, and the great doors are closed. [15b]. The bells of the Castle are again heard. [15a]. The daylight wanes. At the loudest cry of agony uttered by Amfortas during the preceding scene, Parsifal clutched at his own heart convulsively and remained in that position for some time. He now stands rigid as if benumbed. Gurnemanz advances ill-humouredly towards him, and shakes him by the arm.)

GURNEMANZ.

Why do you still stand there? Do you understand what you have seen? [7.]

(Parsifal clutches at his heart convulsively and then shakes his head slightly.) [3.]

GURNEMANZ.

(Very angrily.)

You are after all then nothing but a Fool? [7.]

(Opening a narrow door at the side.)

Get out there, go your own way! [14.] But Gurnemanz advises you: in future leave our swans in peace, [10b] and, gander as you are, seek a goose for yourself!

(He pushes Parsifal out and peevishly slams the door after him. [7.] He then follows the Knights.)

VOICE FROM ABOVE.

By pity enlightened, the stainless Fool. [7.]

VOICES FROM THE HEIGHTS.

Blessed in Faith! [4]

# ACT II.

## THE PRELUDE.

*[This Prelude is a preparatory introduction to the kingdom of Pagan sin and sorcery. A stormy movement surges up over which is heard the theme that portrays the furious rage of the Magician Klingsor,* [12] *to whose domain the scene is now transferred. This is succeeded by the mysterious harmonies associated with the occult powers of magical enchantment and spell of sin, such as Klingsor exercised over Kundry, and Kundry upon her victims* [11]. *To these themes are then added the Wail of God* [16] *and the mocking laughter of Kundry,* [8b.] *which rapidly and persistently succeed each other, rising higher and higher in the scale, whilst the theme of the Magician Klingsor* [12] *forms a turbulent accompaniment in the bass. The concentrated blending of these terrific themes and pathetic cries into a passionate outburst of only sixty bars, prepares the hearer for the scene between Klingsor and Kundry with which the Second Act begins.]*

## KLINGSOR'S MAGIC CASTLE.

SCENE.—In the inner roof of a tower open at the top. Side steps lead to the battlements of the tower wall. Darkness in the depth below to which there is a way down from the floor of the stage, that forms part of the fortification wall. Magical implements and necromantic appliances. Klingsor seated on the fortification wall at one side before a metal mirror.

[11.]

KLINGSOR.

The time has come,—already my magic castle entices the Fool whom I see approaching in the distance, shouting like a child! [7. 14.] In a deadly sleep [11] my curse [8b] enthrals her, whose yoke I know how to unbind. Up then! To work.

(He descends rather lower towards the centre and there produces a cloud of smoke which at once fills the back-ground with a bluish vapour. Klingsor again seats himself before the magic implements and calls with mysterious gestures towards the chasm.) [11.]

Arise! Arise! Come to me! Thy master calls thee, [12] nameless one! Eternal she-devil! Rose of Hell! Herodias thou wert, and what beside? Gundryggia there! Kundry here! Come hither! Come hither then! Kundry! Thy master calls: arise. [12].

(In the bluish light rises the sleeping form of Kundry. Half-awakened she utters a terrible cry, as one startled from a deep sleep.) [8b.]

Dost thou awake! Ha! Under my spell thou hast fallen again to-day betimes.

(Kundry utters a piercing cry of anguish which sinks down gradually to a low moan of terror.)

Say, where hast thou been roving again? For shame! Yonder with that pack of knights, where thou lettest thyself be treated like a brute beast? Does it not please thee better to be with me? [18.] When thou hadst entrapped their master for me—ha! ha! the chaste guardian of the Grail,—what hunted thee away again?

KUNDRY.

(In hoarse and broken accents, as though trying to regain the power of speech.)

Ah!—Ah! Deep night—madness. [11.] Oh! —Rage! [8b.] Ah! misery! Sleep—sleep—deep sleep! Death!

KLINGSOR.

Did another awake thee there? Hey?

KUNDRY.

(As before.)

Yes! My curse! [8b.] Oh! Longing, longing! [16.]

KLINGSOR.

Ha! Ha! For the chaste Knights yonder?

KUNDRY.

There—there—I served.

KLINGSOR.

Yes, yes! To atone for the evil thou maliciously broughtest on them? They do not help thee; they can all be bought, if I offer the right price: the firmest yields if he sinks into thy arms: [18] and then he falls a victim to the Lance [3] which I wrested from their Master himself. [12.] The most dangerous One must be confronted to-day: who is protected by the shield of folly. [7. 3.]

KUNDRY.

I—will not!—oh!—oh!

KLINGSOR.

Yes thou wilt, for thou *must.*

KUNDRY.

Thou canst not hold me.

KLINGSOR.

No, but I can force thee.

KUNDRY.

Thou?

KLINGSOR.

Thy Master.

KUNDRY.

By what power?

KLINGSOR.

Ha! Because over me only thou can'st have no influence.

KUNDRY.

(With a shrill laugh.)

Ha! ha! Art thou chaste? [8b.]

KLINGSOR.

(In a rage.)

Why dost thou ask me that, accursed woman?

(Brooding darkly.)

Terrible extremity! Thus now doth the devil laugh at me, because I once strove for that which is holy

[11. 16.] Terrible extremity! Can the torment of irrepressible longing, the fiendish impulse of terrific desire, which I forced to deadly silence [12] within me, loudly laugh and mock me through thee the devil's bride? [8b.] Beware! One man already has repented of his scorn and contempt, that proud one, strong in holiness, who once spurned me, [12] his race succumbed to me, [6] unredeemed shall the pious guardian pine: [4] and soon—I sometimes dream—I shall be guarding the Grail myself. Ha! ha! Did he please thee well, [6] the hero Amfortas, whom I gave thee for a companion in delight?

KUNDRY.

Oh! Misery! Misery! Weak even he! Weak—all! Through my curse all fall with me! [16.] Oh, eternal sleep, only release, how,—how can I gain thee?

KLINGSOR.

Ha! Whoever defies thee could set thee free: [7] try it with the boy who now approaches!

KUNDRY.

I will not!

KLINGSOR.

Now already he mounts to the Castle. [14.]

KUNDRY.

Oh, alas! Alas! Did I awaken for this? Must I? Must? [8b.]

KLINGSOR.

(Who has ascended the tower wall.)

Ha!—He is handsome, the boy!

KUNDRY.

Oh! Oh! Woe to me! [8b.]

KLINGSOR.

(Blowing a horn.)

Ho!—Ye warders! Ho! Knights! Heroes!—Up! Foes are near! [8a.] Ha!—How they storm—to the wall, the silly coxcombs, to protect their fair she-devils! That's right! Courage! Courage! Ha, ha! He's not afraid:—he has wrested the arms from the hero Ferris; and fiercely wields them against the swarm.

(Kundry begins to laugh uncannily.)

His bravery ill suits these louts! [8a.] He has cut off that one's arm,—and the other one's thigh! Ha, ha!—They yield!—They fly; [14] Each carries home a wound! Little do I regret it. May the whole breed of knights destroy each other in the same way! [7.] Ha! How proudly he stands on the rampart! [14.] How the roses laugh on his cheeks, as he stares with childish wonder into the lonely garden! Hey! Kundry!

(Kundry's laughter which had gradually grown more hysterical and ecstatic, at last ended in a convulsive shriek of agony after which she disappeared. The bluish light has gone out, and there is absolute darkness below, contrasting with the brilliant blue sky above the wall.)

What! already at work?—[20a.] Ha, ha! Well I knew the magic which always compels her to serve my will. [12.] You there, my young cockerel, whatever may have been prophecied about you, [7]—you have fallen into my power, too young and stupid:—when once you have been robbed of purity, [7] you will remain devoted to me!

(He sinks quickly with the whole tower; [12] at the same time the magic garden rises up and fills the entire stage. Tropical vegetation, luxuriant splendour of flowers; towards the background a boundary is formed by the battlement of the castle wall, from which project buttresses of the castle building, which is in florid Arabian style, with terraces.

On the wall stands Parsifal, looking down upon the garden in wonder. [14.]

From all sides, out of the garden and the Palace, in confusion, first singly and then in groups, beautiful maidens rush in with increasing numbers. [8a.] They are covered with delicately-coloured draperies carelessly thrown over them, as if they had just been startled out of sleep.)

MAIDENS.

(Coming from the Garden.)

Here! Here was the tumult! Arms! Wild cries!

MAIDENS.

(Coming from the Castle.)

Alas! Vengeance! Up! Where is the culprit?

A FEW MAIDENS.

My beloved is wounded! [17.]

OTHERS.

Where shall I find mine?

OTHERS.

I awoke alone! Whither have they fled?

OTHERS AGAIN.

Within in the hall?—They bleed! alas! Who is the foe?—There he stands! See!—The sword of my Ferris. I saw it, he stormed the Castle.—I heard the master's horn. My hero rushed to the fight, they all came, but his weapon was ready for each. The bold foe! They all fled before him.—You there! You there! Why have you brought such trouble upon us? [17.] May you be cursed, cursed!

(Parsifal leaps down rather lower into the garden, the maidens shrink back startled, and he pauses full of wonder.) [14.]

THE MAIDENS.

Ha! Bold one! Do you dare to come near us? Why did you slay our lovers?

PARSIFAL.

You beautiful children, was I not forced to slay them? [14.] Why they barred my way to you, you pretty ones.

MAIDENS.

Did you want to come to us? Have you seen us before?

PARSIFAL.

Never before have I seen such pretty creatures: if I call you beautiful, would that seem right to you?

MAIDENS.

Then you don't wish to slay us? [17.]

PARSIFAL.

I should not like to do that.

MAIDENS.

And yet you brought so many troubles upon us! Many and great! You slew our playfellows! Who is to play with us now?

PARSIFAL.

I should like to do that.

MAIDENS.

(The Maidens whose astonishment has changed to merriment, now break out into laughter. While Parsifal gradually approaches the excited groups [14] some maidens gradually withdraw unnoticed behind the fence of flowers, in order to complete their floral costume.)

If you want to be nice to us, don't keep so far away! If you won't scold us, we will be nice to you: we do not play for money. We play for the reward of love. And if you would console us then win that pay from us!

THE ADORNED MAIDENS.

(Coming back dressed as flowers.)

Leave the boy alone! He belongs to me! No!—No!—To *me*!—To *me*!—

THE OTHER MAIDENS.

Ha! How deceitful! They have dressed themselves up on the sly!

(They also withdraw and soon return adorned like the others.)

THE MAIDENS.

(Moving with light dancing step round Parsifal and playfully stroking his cheeks and chin.)

Come! Come! You bonny boy! [18a.] Come! Come! Let me bloom for you! To your pleasure and delight will I devote all my loving efforts!

PARSIFAL.

(Standing in the midst of the maidens in quiet content.)

How sweet is your scent! Are you flowers really?

THE MAIDENS.

(As before; sometimes singly, and at other times in combination.)

We are the graces of the garden and its sweet-scented spirits, [18c] in the spring our master gathers us; we grow here in summer and sun, blooming for you in delight. Now be friendly and kind to us! Do not grudge the flowers their pay! If you do not love and caress us, we shall wither and die.

FIRST MAIDEN.

Take me to thy bosom! [18a and b.]

SECOND MAIDEN.

Let me cool thy brow!

THIRD MAIDEN.

Let me stroke thy cheek!

FOURTH MAIDEN.

Let me kiss thy mouth!

FIFTH MAIDEN.

No *me*! I am the fairest!

SIXTH MAIDEN.

No I! My scent is sweeter.

PARSIFAL.

(Gently pushing them away.)

You lovely wild crowd of flowers, if I am to play with you, give me more room! [14, 17.]

MAIDENS.

Why do you scold?

PARSIFAL.

Because you are quarrelling.

MAIDENS.

We only quarrel for *you*. [19.]

PARSIFAL.

Well, don't then!

FIRST MAIDEN.

(To the second one.)

Leave him alone! Look, it is I he wants!

SECOND MAIDEN.

No, I!

THIRD MAIDEN.

No, it is *I* he would rather have!

FOURTH MAIDEN.

No, I!

FIRST MAIDEN.

(To Parsifal.)

Do you drive me away?

SECOND MAIDEN.

Do you shun me?

FIRST MAIDEN.

What, are you afraid of women?

SECOND MAIDEN.

Dare you not trust yourself?

SEVERAL MAIDENS.

How dreadfully timid and cold you are!

OTHER MAIDENS.

Will you allow the butterfly to woo the flowers?

MAIDENS (*1st half*).

Come away from the Fool!

ONE MAIDEN.

I give him up.

OTHERS.

Then leave him to us!

OTHERS.

No, to us! No, to me!—To me too!—Here, here!—

PARSIFAL.

(Half angrily pushing them away and trying to escape.)

Leave off! You wont catch me! [14.]

(Out of a bower of flowers is heard the voice of)

KUNDRY.

Parsifal! [7.] Stay!

(The Maidens cease playing and start back in fear; Parsifal stands spellbound.)

PARSIFAL.

"Parsifal?" [7.] So once when dreaming my mother called me.

KUNDRY.

(Gradually coming into sight.)

Stay here, Parsifal! [7.]—Delight and good fortune greet thee together. [20a.]—You childish paramours, leave him; you fast-fading flowers, he was not meant for you to sport with. [17.] Go home, tend the wounds: many lonely heroes are waiting for you.

THE MAIDENS.

(The frightened maidens regretfully leave Parsifal and return to the Castle.)

Must we leave you! Must we forsake you! [17.]

Ah, how sad! Oh, alas! Alas for the sorrow! We would gladly part from all to be alone with you. [19.] Farewell! You fair one! You proud one! You—Fool!

(At the last word the maidens disappear laughing into the Castle.)

PARSIFAL.

Have I dreamt all this? [7.]

(Parsifal looks timidly round to the side from which the voice came. There has now become visible through the unfolding of the branches a youthful woman of superlative beauty—Kundry, completely transformed, reclining on a floral couch, in light fantastic dress rather Arabian in style.)

PARSIFAL.

(Still standing apart.)

Thou calledst *me*, who have no name?

KUNDRY.

'Twas thee I called, foolish pure one, "Fal parsi," thou pure foolish one, "Parsifal." [7.] So thy father Gamuret, when he died in Arabian land, called to the son whom, locked in his mother's womb, he greeted with this name when dying. To tell thee this I have waited for thee here: what drew thee hither [20a] if it was not a wish to know? [3.] [7.]

PARSIFAL.

I never looked upon nor even dreamed of what I see here now, which fills me with a strange foreboding. Hast thou too blossomed in this grove of flowers? [18b.]

KUNDRY.

No, Parsifal, thou foolish pure one! [11.] Far,—far, from hence is my home! I waited here only that thou mightest find me, I came from far away, where I saw many things. I saw the child upon its mother's breast, its first lisp laughs still in my ear; how the heart-broken Herzeleide laughed too, [20a] when the delight of her eyes shouted in response to her sorrow! Tenderly nestled among soft mosses, she kissed the lovely babe sweetly to sleep; its slumber was guarded by the fear and trouble of a mother's yearning; [20a] the hot dew of its mother's tears awoke it in the morning. She was all tears, a child of sorrow for thy father's love and death: to protect thee from a like fate was to her the highest mandate of duty: far from arms, from the fighting and raging of men she longed to hide and keep thee. She was all sorrow, aye! and fear: never was knowledge to reach thee. Dost thou not even now hear her cry of woe when thou had'st wandered late? Hey! How she laughed with joy when in her search she found thee; and when she caught thee with rage of love in her arms, [20a] wert thou not almost frightened for very kisses?—But her pain thou could'st not see nor the agony she suffered when after a while thou didst not come back, [20b] and she lost all trace of thee: for days and nights she waited, until her wailing sank into silence, pain was dissolved in sorrow, and she prayed for the peace of death; grief broke her heart, and—Herzeleide—died. [20a.]

PARSIFAL.

(Who has listened with increasing emotion, at last sinks down at Kundry's feet overwhelmed with sorrow and remorse.)

Alas! Alas! What have I done? Where have I been? Mother! Sweet darling mother! [20b] That thy son—thy son should murder thee! O fool! Weak, blundering fool! Whither have you wandered, forgetting her, forgetting thee, thee, faithful, dearest mother! [20b.]

KUNDRY.

If thou art still a stranger to suffering, thy heart has never been refreshed by sweet consolation; as-suage the pain and distress which torment thee in the consolation of love!

PARSIFAL.

(Growing more and more melancholy.)

My mother, my mother—I could forget her! [20b] [3]. Ha! how much besides have I forgotten? [3.] What have I ever remembered yet? [3.] Only dull foolishness dwells in me!

KUNDRY,

(Still reclining, bends over Parsifal's head, gently presses her hand upon his brow, and twines her arm confidingly round his neck.)

Confession will turn guilt into repentance; under-standing will turn foolishness into wisdom: learn to know the love which enveloped Gamuret, when Her-zeleide's passion overflowed, inflaming him. [20a.] She who once gave thee flesh and life, before whom death and folly must flee away, she offers thee to-day, in last greeting of a mother's blessing, [20b] the first kiss of love!

(She has bent her head right over his and now presses her lips on his mouth in a long kiss. [11,2,16.]

PARSIFAL.

(Here Parsifal starts up with a gesture of the greatest terror, becomes terribly changed and presses his hands firmly over his heart, as though to keep down a distracting pain.)

Amfortas!—[8b.] The wound!—The wound!—It burns in my heart.—[6.] Oh! Wail! Wail! Terrible Wail! It cries to me from the depths of my heart. [16.] Oh!—Oh! wretched one!—Most miserable one! —I saw the wound bleeding,—now it bleeds in me! [2.]—Here—here! [16.] No! No! [11.] It is not the wound; [6] though its blood may flow on in streams! Here! Here in my heart is the fire! The passionate, terrible longing [11] which pervades and coerces all my senses! Oh!—Torture of love! [16.] How all things vibrate, heave and throb in sinful lust! . . . .

(While Kundry gazes at Parsifal in terror and amazement, he rises into a state of complete exaltation.) [4.]

(Terribly quiet.)

My eyes, as in a trance, are fixed on the Sacred Cup; [4]—the Holy Blood glows; [1]—the divine and most gentle rapture of redemption palpitates through every soul far and wide: [3] only here in my heart the torment will not abate. The Wail of the Saviour [16] now I comprehend the Wail, ah!

The Wail for His polluted sanctuary: "Redeem, rescue Me [1] from hands defiled by guilt!" [2.] Thus did the Wail of God cry in my soul with terrible might. And I? Fool, coward! I hurried away to wild and boyish deeds! [8a.]

(Throws himself despairingly on his knees.)

Redeemer! Saviour! Lord of Grace! How can I, a sinner, atone for my guilt? [3.]

KUNDRY.

(Whose amazement has turned into passionate admiration tries timidly to approach Parsifal.)

Promised hero! Fly from this delusion! Look up and cherish her who comes to thee with love! [21.]

PARSIFAL.

(Still kneeling, gazes vacantly up at Kundry, who bends over him, and goes through all the caressing gestures which he thus describes.)

Aye! This voice! Thus she called to him;—and this look—I recognise it clearly—and this one too, whose smile was so fatal. The lips,—yes,—thus they allured him;—thus her neck bent over him,—thus she proudly raised her head;—thus fluttered her laughing locks, thus her arm twined round his neck—thus her cheek softly caressed him! In league with all the agony of suffering her mouth kissed his salvation from him! [16.] Ha!—This kiss! [11.]

(Parsifal has gradually risen to his feet, and now pushes Kundry from him.)

Corruptress! Away from me! For ever—for evermore away from me!

KUNDRY.

(With intense passion.)

Cruel one! [21.] Since thy heart feels only for the sufferings of others, then let it feel now too for mine! [23.] If thou art a redeemer, what spell hinders thee, cruel one, from uniting with me for my salvation? [21.] From all eternity have I waited for thee, the saviour, ah! So late! [16.] Whom once I boldly mocked.—Oh!—Didst thou but know the cursé, which through sleep and waking, through death and life, [11] pain and laughter [16] tortures me, ever steeled to fresh suffering, unendingly throughout my existence!—I saw—Him [1]—Him [25]—and—laughed [8b.]. . . . [16]. Then His look fell upon me.—Now I seek Him from world to world, once more to meet Him. [16.] In the deepest distress I seem to feel His eye already near, [22] His look already resting on me. [4.]—Then the accursed laughter [8b] comes upon me again:—a sinner sinks into my arms! [6.] Then I laugh—laugh [8b]—cannot weep: only cry, storm, rave, rage, [12] in an ever-recurring night of madness, from which I have but barely awakened repentant.—He for whom I have longed [3] in the agony of death, whom I have recognised, at whom I impotently laughed: let me weep on his breast, [23] let me be united with thee but for one hour, and then, though God and the world cast me off, in thee I shall be saved and redeemed!

PARSIFAL.

For evermore thou wouldst be damned with me,

were I to forget my mission [7] for one hour in the embrace of thy arms!—For thy salvation also am I sent, if thou dost refrain from desire. The consolation which shall end thy suffering, is not drawn from the fountain whence that suffering flows; salvation will never come to thee, until that fountain is dried up within thee. Another spring it is,—aye! A very different one [16] for which I witnessed such distressful longing, there where the brothers torture and mortify their bodies with awful hardships. But who recognises clearly and luminously the true fountain of the only salvation? [5.] Oh, misery! [16.] Flight of all redemption! Oh, enveloping night of the world's delusion: in hot search of the highest salvation to pine for the fountain of damnation! [16.]

KUNDRY.

(In wild exaltation.)

Was it my kiss then [18b] which revealed the world so clearly to thee? [17.] Then would the embrace of all my love [18c] make thee a God! Redeem the world, if that is thy mission: [7]—if this hour make thee a God, then for that let me be eternally damned, for ever leave my wound unhealed.

PARSIFAL.

Redemption, sinful woman, I offer also to thee. [14.]

KUNDRY.

Let me love thee, divine one, then wouldst thou give me redemption too. [17.]

PARSIFAL.

Love and redemption [14] thou shalt have, if thou showest me the way to Amfortas.

KUNDRY.

(Mad with rage.)

Never—shalt thou find him! [8b.] The fallen one, let him perish, the unholy one, who longed for his disgrace, at whom I laughed—laughed—laughed! [8b.] Ha-ha! Why his own Lance [3] struck him!

PARSIFAL.

Who could wound him with the holy weapon?

KUNDRY.

He—He—Who once punished my laughter; His curse, ha! It makes me strong; [8a] against thee thyself I call the weapon, if thou give to the sinner the honour of pity! [17.]—Ha! Madness!—

(Imploringly.)

Pity! Pity for me! [17.] Only one hour mine,—only one hour thine [23]—and thou shalt be conducted on the way!

(She tries to embrace him, and he thrusts her violently away. She rises up in wild frenzy and calls towards the back.)

PARSIFAL.

Away, [8b] unholy woman!

KUNDRY.

Help! Help! Bring help! [17.] Hold this desperate one! Bring help! Bar the ways! Bar the paths!—And if thou fliest hence and findest all the ways in the world, [8a] the way thou seekest, its path thou shalt not find! For roads and ways which sever thee from me, thus I curse them to thee: [12] Wander! Wander!—That wandering spirit whom I know so well—him I give to thee for a guide!

KLINGSOR.

(Has advanced on to the castle wall, and aims the Lance at Parsifal.)

Hold there! I ban thee with the right weapon! [3.] Let the Fool be laid low by his master's Lance!

(He hurls the Lance at Parsifal over whose head it stops floating in the air.)

PARSIFAL.

(He has seized the Lance with his hand and holds it over his head.) [4.]

With this sign I exorcise thy magic: [4.] as I trust that this shall close the wound which thou hast inflicted with it, so may it overthrow thy illusory splendour in sorrow and ruins! [4.]

(He makes the Sign of the Cross with the Lance; and as if by the shock of an earthquake the castle falls into ruins; [12, 17] the garden has quickly withered up and become a desert waste; faded flowers are strewn upon the ground. Kundry has fallen helplessly to the earth with a loud cry.)

PARSIFAL.

(Pausing a moment on his way and turning back to Kundry from the top of the ruined walls.)

Thou knowest where thou canst find me again! [17.]

(He hastens away; Kundry raises herself a little and gazes after him.) [16.]

# ACT III.

---

## THE PRELUDE.

[*The Prelude seems to indicate what has passed since the close of Act II. It opens with a sad theme on the strings* [24] *characterising the melancholy condition to which the brotherhood have sunk through the neglect of Amfortas to fulfil his office. The next theme that appears is a modification of theme No.* 8a, *here used to describe Parsifal's hopeless wanderings in search of the Holy Grail, which gradually gains strength and assumes more and more nearly the shape of the Grail theme* [4,] *until it is harshly interrupted by theme* 8b, *which rushes down its full three octaves. In the rest of the Prelude, themes* 7, 3 *and* 11 *give a picture of the endless struggles Parsifal had to undergo before bringing back the sacred Lance to the Grail brotherhood.*]

**Scene.—An open, fair spring landscape in the domain of the Grail, with flowery meadows rising gently towards the background. The verge of the forest occupies the foreground, and stretches out in rising rocky ground towards the right. In front, at the edge of the wood is a spring, and opposite to this but rather lower a plain hermit's hut built against a rock. Very early morning.**

(Gurnemanz, now very old, clad as a hermit, but with the tunic of the knights of the Grail, comes from the hut and listens.) [17.] [11.]

GURNEMANZ.

The groaning came from that direction. No wild animal wails so piteously, [12] and certainly not on this most holy morning. [29b.] Methinks I know that plaintive wail. [11.]

(He steps resolutely to a thicket of thorn at the side, which has overgrown itself, pushes the branches asunder, and pauses suddenly.)

GURNEMANZ.

Ha! *She* here again? [11.] The rough brambles of winter have kept her concealed: how long? Up!—Kundry!—Up! The winter has fled, and the spring is here! Awake! Awake to the spring!

(He drags the rigid and lifeless form of Kundry from the thicket, and bears her to a grassy mound close by.)

GURNEMANZ.

Cold—and stiff! This time I really think she is dead: and yet it was her groaning which I heard?

(Gurnemanz vigorously rubs the hands and brow of Kundry, as she lies stretched out rigidly before him, and spares no effort to relax her stiffness. At last life seems to awake in her. [17.] She awakens completely, and as she opens her eyes [17, 4]—gives forth a cry. [8b.])

(Kundry is in a coarse penitent's dress as in the first Act; her complexion is paler, and the wildness has vanished from her appearance and manner. She gazes for a long time at Gurnemanz. Then she rises, arranges her dress and hair, and at once sets to work like a serving maid.) [8c.]

GURNEMANZ.

You mad woman! Have you no word for me? Are

these your thanks to me for once more waking you from the sleep of death ?

KUNDRY.

(Slowly bowing her head and then murmuring in hoarse and broken accents.)

Let me serve . . . serve ! [8c.]

GURNEMANZ.

(Shaking his head.)

That will give you but little trouble ! Messages are sent no more; herbs and roots each one finds for himself, we learnt it in the forest from the animals.

(Kundry meanwhile has looked around her, and perceiving the hut enters it. Gurnemanz gazes after her in astonishment.)

GURNEMANZ.

How different this to her usual gait ! Is this a work of this sacred day ? [4.] Oh ! transcendent day of grace ! [25.] Doubtless for her salvation [3] I was allowed to-day to arouse this poor creature from her sleep of death.

(Kundry comes again from the hut, carrying a water pitcher, and bears it to the spring. Looking hence towards the wood she sees in the distance some one approaching, and turns to Gurnemanz to point this out to him. [29a.])

GURNEMANZ.

Who comes towards the holy well there ? [26.] In dusky armour ? That is not one of the brothers !

(During the following entrance of Parsifal Kundry slowly retires into the hut with the pitcher, which she has filled, and there finds work to do. Parsifal enters from the wood ; he is completely arrayed in black armour ; with closed helmet and lowered Lance; he walks slowly along dreamily hesitating, and seats himself on the little knoll of grass. [26.])

GURNEMANZ.

(Having observed Parsifal with astonishment advances towards him.)

Hail to you, my guest! Have you lost your way, and shall I set you right? [26.]

(Parsifal gently shakes his head.)

Do you offer me no salutation in return?

(Parsifal bows his head.)

Hey! What? If your oath binds you to keep silence with me, mine obliges me to tell you what is befitting. Here you are in a sacred place [4]: one comes not here with weapons, with closed helmet, shield and lance; and to-day too! Do you not know what a holy day this is? [4, 25.]

(Parsifal shakes his head.)

From whence then do you come? With what heathen have you sojourned that you know not to-day is the all-hallowed Good Friday? [25.]

(Parsifal sinks his head yet lower.)

Quick, off with your weapons! Do not offend the Lord, Who to-day, naked of all defence, offered His Holy Blood [3] as an atonement for the sinful world!

(After a further silence Parsifal rises, thrusts the Lance upright into the earth before him, and lays beside it his sword, and shield, and spear, opens his helmet which he takes from his head and lays with the other weapons, and then kneels down in silent prayer before the Lance. Gurnemanz regards him with wonder and emotion. He beckons Kundry, who has again come forth from the hut. [25.] Parsifal now raises his eyes reverently to the point of the Lance. [3]).

GURNEMANZ.

(Softly to Kundry.)

Do you recognise him? It is he who once laid low the swan. [1.]

(Kundry nods assent, and gazes fixedly and calmly on Parsifal.)

Undoubtedly 'tis he, [3] the Fool, whom angrily I sent away from us. [1.]

Ha! what path did he find? [3, 16, 7.] The Lance—I know it. [7, 3.]

(With deep emotion.)

Oh! Holiest day on which I was fated to open my eyes! [16.]

(Kundry has turned her face away.)

PARSIFAL.

(Parsifal rises slowly from prayer, looks calmly around him, and recognising Gurnemanz extends his hand to him tenderly in greeting. [25, 4.])

Happy I, that I find you again!

GURNEMANZ.

Do you then know me still? Do you recognise me bowed as I am so low by grief and care? [24.] How came you to-day, and whence?

PARSIFAL.

By paths of error and of suffering I came; [8a.] am I to deem my wanderings over and feel that my struggle is at an end, now that I hear once more this murmuring of the forest [10a], and greet you again, you good old man? Or—must I wander further? Everything seems to me changed.

GURNEMANZ.

Then say, to *whom* have you been seeking the way?

PARSIFAL.

To him, whose bitter wail I listened to once in foolish amazement, [6,7] to whom I may now consider myself chosen to bring salvation. [3, 7.] But—ah!—a wild curse has driven me about in pathless wanderings, never to find the way of salvation [24, 8a.]; countless troubles, struggles, conflicts forced me from the path, when I thought I had already recognised it aright. Then did despair seize me of keeping safe the holy thing [3, 7], to guard which I received wounds from every weapon; for it itself I might not wield in combat; undefiled I bore it at my side, the weapon which now I carry home [4], and which gleams so bright and beautiful before you, the holy Lance of the Grail. [1.]

GURNEMANZ.

(Breaking out into the most intense rapture.)

O grace! Highest salvation! [25.] Oh! marvel! Holy, most glorious marvel! [3.] [13.]

(After he has somewhat controlled himself, to Parsifal.)

Oh, my Lord! If it was a curse which drove you from the right path, believe me, it is gone. You are here, this is the Grail's domain [4]; its knighthood wait for you. Ah, it needs salvation, the salvation which you bring! Since the day on which you came here, the sorrow you then perceived, the fear, has grown to the highest pitch [24.]. Amfortas, [6] to get rid of the torture of his wound and of his soul, [16, 8b.] implored in raging defiance for death. No prayers, nor yet the misery of his knights could persuade him to fulfil the holy office any more. [24.] The Grail has remained for a long time locked in its shrine: and in this way its sin-repentant guardian hopes, as he cannot die if he ever looks upon it, to force on his end, and finish his torture with his life. The holy food now remains denied to us, common fare must nourish us: on this account our heroes' strength is exhausted [24.]: messages come no more to us nor calls to holy wars from afar: pale and miserable the knights wander about, without courage or leader. [24.] In this forest corner I have hidden myself, calmly waiting for death, to which my old commander has already succumbed, for Titurel, my holy hero, [9] whom now the sight of the Grail [4] no more refreshed, he died,—a man like all! [24.]

PARSIFAL.

(With a gesture of despair.)

And I,—'tis I, who have worked all this misery! Ha! What guilt of sin and crime must weigh down this Fool's head from everlasting, since no repentance, no atonement frees me of my blindness, I myself chosen out as a saviour, [7] hopelessly lost in error, the last path of salvation vanishes from me!

(Parsifal is about to fall into a faint, Gurnemanz holds him erect, and supports him into a sitting posture on to the knoll of grass. Kundry hastens to bring a basin of water to sprinkle him.)

GURNEMANZ.

(Waving Kundry away.) [23.]

Not so! The holy well itself must refresh our pilgrim's bath. [27.] I think he has yet to accomplish a high work to-day, to fulfil a holy office [4] : so let him be free from stains [28a], and the dust of long wandering in error shall now be washed away from him.

(They both lead Parsifal gently to the edge of the spring. While Kundry loosens his greaves, and bathes his feet, and Gurnemanz takes off his corslet, [28b] Parsifal asks.)

PARSIFAL.

(Gently and wearily.)

Shall I to-day be conducted to Amfortas?

GURNEMANZ.

(Still attending upon Parsifal.)

Most assuredly the fair castle awaits us : [30] the sepulture of my beloved master calls me there myself. Amfortas now promises that he will once more unveil to us the Grail, once again fulfil his holy office [4], in sanctification of his noble father, who died the victim of his son's guilt, for which that son would thus atone.

PARSIFAL.

(Watching Kundry in astonishment.) [22.]

You have washed my feet [28a], now let my friend besprinkle my head.

GURNEMANZ.

(Taking some water into his hand from the spring and pouring it over Parsifal's head.)

Blessed be thou, pure one through this pure water! [27.] So may the sorrow of all sin depart from thee! [28b.]

(Meanwhile Kundry has taken a golden phial from her bosom, and poured a portion of its contents over Parsifal's feet, and dries them with her hair, which she has quickly unbound.) [27, 25, 17.]

PARSIFAL.

(Gently taking the phial from Kundry and handing it to Gurnemanz.)

You have anointed my feet [17], now let the companion of Titurel anoint my head, that to-day he may yet hail me as King.

GURNEMANZ.

(During the ensuing words Gurnemanz pours the whole contents of the flask over Parsifal's head, and gently rubs it, and then folds his hands over it.)

So was it promised to us; so do I bless thy head, [14]—and hail thee as king. Thou—pure one—compassionate sufferer, enlightened deliverer! [7.] As thou hast borne the sufferings of the redeemed one, so now take the last burden from his head. [4.]

PARSIFAL.

(Who unperceived has taken water into his hand from the spring, bends down towards Kundry who is still kneeling and sprinkles it over her head.)

My first duty I fulfil thus [27]: be baptised, and believe on the Redeemer! [5.]

(Kundry bows her head to the earth, and appears to weep bitterly.) [16]

PARSIFAL.

(Turning and gazing in gentle ecstacy upon woods and plains which gleam in the light of morning.) [29a.]

How beautiful the meadows seem to me to-day!

[29a.] I once met with magic flowers, which climbing up to my head eagerly sought to clasp me; but never saw I the grass, and flowers, and blossoms, so sweet and tender, nor ever smelled they so childishly pure, nor ever spoke to me with such loving confidence. [29b.]

GURNEMANZ.

That, Lord, is the magic of Good Friday!

PARSIFAL.

Oh, alas for that day of deepest agony! [1.] Then surely, all that blossoms, breathes, lives and lives again, ought to mourn, ah! and weep? [2, 5.]

GURNEMANZ.

Thou see'st, that is not so. [29a.] It is the contrite tears of sinners [28] which to-day with holy dew besprinkle field and meadow: it has made them so fresh and blooming. [4.] Now all created things rejoice at the Redeemer's holy trace, and to Him would consecrate their prayers. [29a.] Himself upon the cross they cannot see, and so they look up to redeemed man, [3] who feels himself free from the burden and horror of sin, and made pure and whole through God's sacrifice of love; and the grass and flowers in the meadows are mindful that on this day they are untrodden by the foot of man, because just as God with divine patience had pity on him and suffered for him, so man also to-day with pious care spares them with gentle tread. For this do all created things give thanks, all that blossoms and quickly fades, since ransomed nature gained this morn her day of innocence.

(Kundry who has slowly raised her head, looks up beseechingly to Parsifal, her eyes filled with tears.) [29b.]

PARSIFAL.

I saw them wither, who once laughed to me; [17] thinkest thou that to-day *they* long for redemption? [16.] Thy tears have also become a dew of blessing: thou weepest, see the meadow smiles. [29a.]

(He gently kisses her upon the brow. The bells of Monsalvat are now heard.) [15b, 30a.]

GURNEMANZ.

Mid-day: the hour has come. Permit Lord, that thy servant may conduct thee!

(Gurnemanz has brought from the hut his Knight's mantle, with which he and Kundry invest Parsifal. Parsifal solemnly grasps the Lance, and with Kundry follows Gurnemanz who slowly leads. [14.]—The landscape is changed very gradually just as in Act I., only from right to left.—After remaining visible for some time the three disappear entirely, as the wood is gradually lost to view, giving place to vaults of rocks.—In vaulted passages, the ringing of bells growing ever louder and louder. The walls of rock open out and the great hall of the Grail is again disclosed to view, as in Act I., only without the refectory tables.—Gloomy light.—From one side enter knights carrying Titurel's corpse in a coffin, from the opposite side other knights carry Amfortas on his litter, in front of whom is borne the draped shrine of the Grail.)

[*The solemn music accompanying the moving scenery and the passing of Gurnemanz, Parsifal and Kundry to the Hall of the Holy Grail, begins with theme No.* 30a, *the funeral march of King Titurel, with which are associated themes* 20b *and* 24. *These are followed by theme No.* 30b, *a new subject founded upon No.* 15a, *which ultimately gives place to No.* 24 *as the great hall of the Grail comes into view.*]

FIRST TRAIN OF KNIGHTS.

(With Amfortas.)

As we transport the Grail to the Holy Office in its hiding shrine, whom is it that in gloomy shrine ye bear along mourning? [30a.]

SECOND TRAIN OF KNIGHTS.

(With Titurel's body.)

The shrine of mourning hides the hero; it conceals the holy power into whose keeping God once gave Himself; Titurel we bear along. [30a.]

FIRST TRAIN OF KNIGHTS.

Who laid him low, him who in God's grace once protected God Himself?

SECOND TRAIN OF KNIGHTS.

The conquering burden of age laid him low, when he no longer looked upon the Grail.

FIRST TRAIN OF KNIGHTS.

Who hindered him from looking on the succour of the Grail?

SECOND TRAIN OF KNIGHTS.

He whom ye transport there, its sinful guardian.

FIRST TRAIN OF KNIGHTS.

We conduct him to-day because he will once more for the last time perform his office.

(Amfortas has now been set down upon the couch behind the Grail table, and the coffin in front of it. The knights turn towards Amfortas with the following words.)

THE KNIGHTS.

Ah, for the last time! Alas! Thou guardian of the Grail! Be mindful of thine office! [30b.]

AMFORTAS.

(Wearily raising himself a little.)

Aye,—Alas! Alas! Alas for me! In that cry I willingly join you. Still more willingly would I accept death from you, the gentlest atonement for sin! [24.]

(The coffin is opened. At the sight of Titurel's body the knights utter a cry of lamentation.)

AMFORTAS.

(Raising himself from his couch and addressing the corpse of Titurel.)

My father! Most blessed among heroes! [31a.] Thou purest one, to whom angels once bowed themselves: I who alone desired to die, to thee I gave death! Oh! Thou who now in divine splendour dost behold the Redeemer Himself, [13] implore of Him that His Holy Blood, [25] if once more its blessing is to refresh the brothers, [1] may at length give death to me, as it imparts new life to them! Death! To die:—only mercy! [31b.] Let the terrible wound, the poison, die; let it deaden the heart at which it gnaws! My father! To thee I cry! Cry thou to Him, "Redeemer, give my son *rest*!"

FIRST TRAIN OF KNIGHTS.

(Pressing nearer to Amfortas.)

Perform thine office! Thou must!

SECOND TRAIN OF KNIGHTS.

Unveil the Grail! Thy father reminds thee; thou *must!* [30b.]

AMFORTAS.

(Leaping up in a paroxysm of despair, and rushing down amongst the recoiling knights.)

Never again! Ha! [6.] Already I feel death darkening around me, and am I to return to life again? Madmen! Who will force me to live? If you could only give me death!

(Tearing open his garment.)

Here I am! Here is the open wound! Here flows my blood which poisons me. Out with your weapons! [12.] Thrust your swords deep, deep, right down to the hilt! Up! Ye heroes! Kill the tortured sinner, and then the Grail will glow for you of its own accord! [4.]

(All have shrunk back in fear from Amfortas who now stands alone in a terrible ecstacy. Parsifal, accompanied by Gurnemanz and Kundry, has come in among the knights unobserved; he now steps forward, stretches forth the Lance, with the point of which he touches Amfortas' side.)

PARSIFAL.

Only one weapon can avail! [4.] Only the Lance which opened the wound can close it. [3.]

(The countenance of Amfortas glows with holy rapture, and he is about to stagger from intense emotion; Gurnemanz supports him.)

PARSIFAL.

Be whole, purified, and redeemed! [6] For I now perform thine office. Blessed be thy suffering, which gave the highest power of pity, and the strength of purest knowledge to the timid Fool. [7.]

(He marches to the centre and raises the Lance aloft before him.) [14.]

The holy Lance, I bring it back to you! [1.]

(All gaze in rapture on the uplifted Lance, whilst Parsifal with his eyes bent upon its point, continues as if inspired.) [13.]

Oh! what a miracle of highest bliss! [13.] From the Lance which closed thy wound I see the Holy Blood flowing, [3] in ardent longing for the sister-fountain, [16] which floweth in the wave of the Grail. No more shall it be veiled. Unveil the Grail! Open the shrine! [1.]

(Parsifal mounts the steps of the altar, takes the Grail from the shrine which has been already opened by the youths, and at the sight of it falls on his knees in silent prayer. [4. 5.] The Grail gradually glows with a soft light.—Increasing darkness below as the light from the height grows brighter.)

THE KNIGHTS AND VOICES FROM THE HEIGHT.

Miracle of highest redemption! [7.]
Redemption to the Redeemer! [1] [5] [4.]

(Ray of light; most intense glowing of the Grail.—A white dove floats down from the dome and hovers over Parsifal's head. Kundry with her eyes bent upwards towards Parsifal, sinks slowly to the ground before him, dead.—Amfortas and Gurnemanz kneel in homage before Parsifal, who waves the Grail in benediction over the adoring knighthood.)

(THE CURTAIN SLOWLY DESCENDS.)

# THE
# MUSICAL THEMES.

# THE MUSICAL THEMES.

[1.]

To these phrases are sung the words :—"Take unto you My Body, take unto you My Blood ; the symbol of our Love." "Take unto you My Blood, take unto you My Body, in remembrance of Me." The sacred import of these words determines the dramatic association of the themes, which constantly recur throughout the drama.

[2.]

This figure forms a portion of Theme No. I., but is used independently. It is like a sigh of pain, and is used, for example, where Parsifal clutches at his heart to repress the agony caused by the kiss of Kundry.

[3.]

This phrase is almost identical with the cadence of Theme No. I, but is used independently. The first four notes constantly accompany a definite reference to the Sacred Lance, and the whole phrase is associated directly or mystically with the Lance, or with the suffering caused by it, or generally with fellow-feeling and pity for pain. For example, Gurnemanz's first mention of the "Wondrous Lance emblazoned with the Precious Blood;" or, when Parsifal kneels in prayer gazing up at the Lance; or, when Parsifal's pity is awakened for the dead swan.

[4.]

This theme is an ancient response still in use at the Catholic Church at Dresden. It occurs constantly throughout the drama, always in connection with the Holy Grail.

[5.]

This is the theme of Faith, and is sung to the words, " Faith lives ; the Dove hovers, the Saviour's Holy Messenger : receive the wine which flows for you, and partake of the Bread of Life." Two other significant applications of this theme should be noticed, one when Parsifal, enlightened by pity, yet hesitates as to the true source of salvation, and says, " But who recognises clearly and distinctly the true source of the only salvation ? " The other where Parsifal says to Kundry, " Baptised be thou, and believe in the Redeemer."

[6.]

This phrase is always used in connection with the wounded Amfortas.

[7.]

This theme accompanies the words of prophecy:—
"By pity enlightened, the stainless Fool: wait for

him, my chosen One." It is elsewhere always found in association with references to the mission of the simple innocent Parsifal, as the promised deliverer.

[8.]

This bounding figure is developed into a wild galloping movement which culminates in the following passage:—

This music which accompanies Kundry's first appearance, and depicts her roving, her mocking laughter, and generally her wild impulsive passionate nature, is associated with these aspects of her character throughout the drama.

This music is associated with two examples of the better aspects of Kundry's character and her desire to atone through service. In Act I. it accompanies her gift of the healing balsam brought from Arabia for Amfortas. In Act III. it accompanies her desire to "serve." In both cases it immediately follows theme 8b.

A heroic phrase suggested by theme No. 5 which accompanies allusions to King Titurel and the chivalry of the Knights, inspired by their ***faith.***

[10.]

This graceful melody describes the morning murmur of the forest leaves. It is employed during the scene in the woodland glade in Act I., and accompanies Parsifal's reference to the murmuring forest in Act III.

Harmonies associated with the swan, which occur in Lohengrin in the same connection.

[11.]

These mysterious harmonies are associated with the enchantment of magic, and the spell of sin. They portray the occult power of Klingsor over Kundry, and the evil spell exercised by her in the ruin of Amfortas as he lay entranced in her arms; also her temptation of Parsifal in the burning kiss.

[12.]

This wild theme portrays the furious and diabolical rage of the magician Klingsor.

[13.]

SOLENNE.

Der zen - gen - gü - ter höck - stes

*pp*

Wun - der gut, das ga - ben die in

*pp*

The melody of this theme is derived from Theme No. 5, but its harmonies irresistibly suggest the mystical and supernatural ideas with which it is always associated. For example, where it accompanies the account of the divine messengers bringing the Grail to King Titurel, quoted above; or, where the uplifted Lance glows with the Precious Blood.

[14.]

The heroic theme of Parsifal indicating his physical prowess as a youth, and his moral triumph over the powers of sin.

[15.]

These four notes rung upon the bells of the Castle of Monsalvat, summon the Brotherhood to the exposition of the Holy Grail. They are afterwards developed upon the orchestra into a rhythmical accompaniment

to the hymn sung by the knights as they march into the refectory.

[16.]

The pathetic anguish of this piercing cry, carries direct to the heart the Wail of the Crucified God. It is associated primarily with the sorrow of God for the sin of the world, and the consequent passion to redeem; and conjointly with all human co-operation with that sorrow, and ensuing passion to be redeemed. It is associated with the reference made by Amfortas to the Lance which pierced the Saviour's wound, "from whence with tears of Blood the Divine One wept with holy, longing pity, for the disgrace of mankind." This theme helps to convey to the soul one of the deepest mystical truths of the story, and it therefore pervades the whole drama either in its melodic or harmonic form.

[17.]

This chromatic phrase first accompanies the lamentations of the flower-maidens for their slain and wounded lovers, and throughout the scene in the magic garden is generally allied with the yearnings of disappointed desire. In the third Act its torm is more dignified, and its mission is to accompany allusions to the desire for redemption in those who once revelled in Klingsor's garden.

der.....
Kna - - be
C.
Wir
wach - - - - - - - - - - - -
sen.....
hier...........................

These seductive melodies express the caressing endearments of the flower-maidens, when they surround Parsifal in the enchanted garden, singing and dancing.

[19.]

This sprightly movement depicts the squabbling of the Flower Maidens, as they hustle each other in rivalry for Parsifal, as well as his own impatience at their importunate teasing.

[20.]

These are the two themes connected with Herzeleide. The first is descriptive of her sorrowful story, and the second of Parsifal's bitter self-reproach at his neglect of her.

[21.]

This figure recurs constantly throughout Kundry's

attempt to captivate Parsifal by means of caresses and endearments.

[22.]

This succession of harmonies occurs twice only in the drama; once in the second Act, where Kundry speaks of the Saviour's pitying look which fell upon her, and which she seeks to meet again: and the second time in the third Act when she bathes Parsifal's feet, and he gazes upon her in compassionate wonder.

[23.]

This emphatic passage accompanies the last desperate appeal of Kundry to Parsifal during the temptation scene, when she completely abandons herself to union with him regardless of all possible consequences. It recurs during the third Act in the orchestra, when Kundry, in abject devotion, brings water to refresh the fainting Parsifal.

[24.]

This melancholy theme which pervades the third Act, describes the attenuated condition to which the brotherhood of Monsalvat has been reduced, through the refusal of Amfortas to unveil the Holy Grail.

[25.]

These piercing harmonies are used throughout the drama in connection with any allusion to Good Friday as the commemoration of our Lord's Passion. This phrase is based upon theme No. 2.

[26.]

This music accompanies Parsifal's appearance in Act III. It is his original heroic theme [14], but transformed, and combined with a new figure in the bass, which is also used independently to describe his intense weariness, his halting gait, and his hopeless wanderings from the right path.

[27.]

This solemn phrase occurs when Gurnemanz baptises Parsifal, and when Parsifal baptises Kundry.

[28.]

A.

B.

These two melodies accompany the scene of the washing of Parsifal's feet, and his purification.

These exquisite Melodies are associated with references to the divine magic of Good Friday, which makes the fields and meadows gleam with heavenly light and beauty.

These themes form the funeral march of King Titurel.

[31.]

These themes accompany the prayer of Amfortas when he pleads before his dead father for his intercession with the Saviour

# THE MYSTERY.

# THE MYSTERY.

---

PARSIFAL is rightly called a "mystery" drama, because it displays, by means of allegory and symbol, the secret of redeeming love. And, in order to deepen our sympathy with this sublime theme, the poet has marshalled the magic powers of music, so that the veil of the visible drama is woven with subtle threads of tone, which give existence in our souls to properties and qualities in men and things that cannot be expressed in act or word.

## THE TWO KINGDOMS.

The allegory commences by revealing to us an ideal mystic community of Knights founded by King Titurel, whose office it is to guard the Holy Grail and the Sacred Lance, and to succour the weaker brethren of the household of faith when persecuted by the kingdom of the world. These knights are chosen on account of their purity, and their vocation is not only to continence, but to that stainless chastity which operates as a redeeming counsel of perfection. Miraculously nourished by the glowing Grail these militant champions of the citadel of faith are inspired to deeds of Christian chivalry. Their home is a consecrated enclosure to which no unclean soul can find the path, where they live as it were in sight of the supernatural. In that domain even animal life is held sacred, and the aspect of nature is pure and peaceful, with cool woodland glades, calm lake, and clear spring.

This sanctuary may be taken as a type of the Kingdom of God amongst men, a radiant centre giving out the light and heat of faith and love. Under the serene patriarchate of King Titurel it pictures the golden age of faith, the spiritual Utopia which always has been, and is to be. The aged monarch himself is a type of the best humanity of that age, full of faith and love. His one cry was, "Reveal the Grail," for to him this sublime symbol was light and life, and when it was withheld he died.

The story of the suppression of the Holy Grail has been already told in the tragic narrative of this drama. The magician Klingsor, an unsuccessful postulant for the Grail community, disqualified by sin and soured by envy, established a rival community. Equipped with occult powers, he furnished his domain with the seductive pleasures of sin, in order to entrap and destroy Titurel's knights, and thus gradually gain possession of the Grail and the Lance. One after another he allured his victims until he finally inveigled Titurel's son Amfortas, the hereditary royal guardian of the Grail, from whom he stole the Lance, and with it gave the wound which nothing would heal.

The enchanted domain of Klingsor is a figure of

the kingdom of this world, manifesting the Pagan pride of life. Called into existence by magic, the "baseless fabric" of its "insubstantial pageant" vanished before the sign of the cross. This illusion of enchantment is a type of all evil, which has no existence of itself, but is only the negation, perversion, or corruption of that which has existence. The equipment of the enchanted garden consisted of those evanescent phenomena which blind the heart and the true aim of life, not because all of them are necessarily wrong in themselves, but because they are so apt to become the chief objects of existence, and in this manner turn the soul away from God, its only end. In this garden an imperfect answer was given to the "wherefore" of existence. The men were filled with an envious appetite for ascendancy, the women with love of admiration, and both sexes with lust and luxury. All were under the dominion of *desire,* at one moment craving, at another complaining. The frivolous coquettes, types of that physical beauty "whose action is no stronger than a flower," displayed all the vacant vanity induced by a life consecrated to enjoyment. All they asked for was someone to play with, and they were ready, at a moment's notice, to transfer their allegiance from their wounded lovers to the new comer who had injured them. Even Klingsor himself betrays an imperfect and distorted judgment, by matching his own cunning against the witless inexperience of Parsifal, making no allowance for the strength of instincts and intuitions in a chaste and sympathetic heart. The rank, gaudy, tropical foliage of the garden may be taken as a figure of the "lying pomp" of sin's illusion.

### Amfortas.

It was in this garden that Amfortas lost the Sacred Lance, and with it his own peace of mind and health of body. The tragic and pathetic figure of the wounded king may be regarded as the type of all favoured souls who are struck down by the evil one, and disfigured by the lasting stigmata of sin. He was born to great spiritual estate, and endowed by inheritance with the highest gifts of grace. To him was given the custody and exposition of the holiest symbols on earth, ordained to be guarded by clean hands and pure hearts. Overcome by spiritual pride, he bargained away heavenly treasure for earthly vanity, and his downfall was in proportion to the loftiness of his original estate. His wound, which would not heal, is a figure of the ever open sore of conscience unappeased. The sting of his sin was the thought of privileges parted with for a mess of potage, of eternal good bartered for temporal illusion. He was given up to remorse and self-reproach, and wanted to abandon the sacred office of unveiling the Grail, longing for the release of death. Thus are the springs of action weakened by despair, for hopeless souls lose all confidence in good works. With such men sacraments and symbols avail nothing, except to swell the torrent of bitter self-reproach. In the utter helplessness of Amfortas we find some measure of his guilt. It is the office of man to rule and order in the state or the family, and he who is paralysed by shame at his own sin, is like one wounded by the powers of evil, whose impotence thwarts the purposes of his Maker, and the well-being of his neighbour. The ruin of Amfortas beggared the whole community of which he was brother-in-chief. Deprived of the Grail the knights lost all power to perform deeds of Christian chivalry, retaining only the faith which, without works, is dead.

The redemption of this self-abased, God-abandoned sinner, is the theme of the drama, and the vocation of its hero Parsifal. It is a repetition of the allegory of the Prodigal Son. The salvation of Amfortas began in his own soul. Kneeling before the plundered and polluted sanctuary he bewailed his own outcast state, and turned to God for healing. Overcome by the sense of sin he became possessed by the sorrow which seeks redemption. This passion for salvation once conceived within the heart, gives a supernatural energy to the human will by uniting it with the will divine. Amfortas turned from self to God, and the work of redemption at once began, for it has been promised that those who hunger and thirst after righteousness shall be filled. From out the glowing chalice of the Grail came the prophecy of a deliverer, stainless and simple, whom God had selected, and for whom the sinner was to wait. He it was who should regain by merit the grace which

Amfortas had received by inheritance, and lost through concupiscence.

As Titurel is a type of the past golden age of loving faith, so Amfortas represents the present iron age of loveless doubt. The symbol was in his hands, but his one cry was "leave it unrevealed." Yet all our sympathies go out to this wounded human sinner, so full of veneration for the age gone by, so full of sorrow for his own state, so wistfully waiting for the deliverer in the age that is to be.

### Parsifal.

Parsifal is the divinely appointed deliverer. He is the child of Gamuret, who died a violent death before the boy was born, and Herzeleide, or *heart's affliction*. This parentage is a type of uredeemed human society as we now see it, the salvation of which is to be wrought by the saviour of the future, born of the sorrow of to-day; so that Parsifal becomes a figure of the redeemed society which is to be. To fit him for his vocation he is brought up in perfect innocence, "unstained by sorrow and unsoiled by sin." He is reared apart from the world, abstemiously, and ignorant of desire and its gratification. By this means the best natural intuitions and instincts given by God remain unpoisoned and unfettered. How this stainless innocence was to be shaped into an effective instrument of salvation for others, is the problem of the drama.

To accomplish this the dramatist has devised a

series of incidents by which this innocent soul is gradually seized of pity, and of the knowledge born of pity, and thus comprehends the purpose of life through sympathy, and not through corruption. The unpolluted soul, educated by compassion, thus becomes as it were a clean lancet in the skilled hand of the surgeon, fitted to relieve the imposthume of selfish sin. But the saving hero must be sheltered from "the slings and arrows of outrageous fortune," the poison of sorrow, and the venom of sin. He must even be deprived of food that might accidentally poison him. He must never know the corrosion generated by the contact of the soul with sin and suffering. His moral nerve must never be shattered by the shock of despairing remorse. The acids of human experience must be used to generate outgoing currents of pity and understanding, for so long as the force flows freely away, inward corrosion is averted. No energy is lost or strength wasted, by the most generous transference of unselfish love, unconsumed by desire, and unravaged by remorse. It is the innocent soul kept unspotted from the world, which generates the undefiled religion that tends the fatherless and the widows. And this stainless, innocent inexperience is that foolishness of the world which is wisdom with God. Guileless natures are ever open to divine sympathies. It was the *Lamb* of God Who took away the sin of the world. It is the little child who is most readily called into the Kingdom of God. Purity is the soil in which love grows free and strong; not the love of *desire*, but that which "pours itself into its brothers and lives for them alone:" which loses life that it may gain it: which asks no recompense from beauty, no reward from the senses, no return from intellect, no wage of wealth or honour, but seeks only to satisfy that hunger to redeem, the divine instinct in hearts capable of pity.

As Titurel represents the golden age of Loving Faith, and Amfortas the present iron age of loveless doubt, so Parsifal is a type of the coming Utopia, in which a new generation, born of sorrow, and therefore shielded from pain and sin, shall learn through fellow-feeling the secret of redeeming love, and shall restore the symbols of faith to those from whom they have been stolen and withheld.

The story of Parsifal's life may also be taken as an allegory of the wonderful designs of Providence concerning the soul of man in relation to the mystery of existence, its concealed purpose, and its hidden God. Parsifal is the chosen child of Providence gradually educated for his mission by the environment through which he is divinely guided. He begins his work unconscious of what it is to be, and ignorant of what it is to do. Indeed, he never fully recognises his mission until it is well nigh completed. He first enters the Grail's domain, an aimless, thoughtless boy, attracted by the outward aspects of chivalry, "the glittering men on beautiful animals:" and so little conscious is he, or those he is about to serve, of the high mission preordained for him, that he is ignominiously turned out as a hopeless fool. The enchanted towers of the Castle of Evil attract him next, and these he seeks as a child would a toy, not knowing that the sacred Lance is there, or that he is about to recover it. Even when this is accomplished, and after years of wandering and struggle he returns to the Grail's domain, he is surprised to find himself there. As he works out his destiny, the various events and characters around him are projected into a divinely-disposed drama of life, of which he has neither initiated the plot nor chosen the *dramatis personæ.* Up to the end he attempts no diagnosis of life and its problems, constructs no theories, offers no criticism of the hidden purposes of the Most High, he only opens his heart to pity, closes it to lust, and leaves the rest to God. He begins by being recognised as a fool, he ends by being acknowledged as a conqueror. He is the foolish thing chosen to confound the wise, the weak thing chosen to confound the strong. The secret of his strength is his sympathy with suffering. In the moment of his great temptation and still greater renunciation, surrounded with every sensual delight that Pagan enchantment could suggest, his whole soul reeling with the intoxicating delirium of sinful longing, his burning lips embittered by the fruit of the tree of knowledge of good and evil, Parsifal turned the pity of his sympathetic heart towards the wounded Amfortas, and from Amfortas to the crucified God upon the hill of Calvary. From the secret depths of his soul there rang out a bitter cry of anguish, an echo of the Wail of God for the sin of fallen man. With that divine lamentation he united every faculty of his being, and in the strength of that co-operation became more than conqueror.

In the long wandering and struggles endured by Parsifal through the curse of Kundry, between his recovery of the Sacred Lance and his return to the Grail's domain, we have a figure of the probation which tests the perseverance of chosen heroes, and an instance of how the vilest instruments are used to display the greatest triumphs of grace. It was through much tribulation that Parsifal came into the Kingdom of God. This trial called out the noblest qualities in his character, not only his zeal and perseverance, but his generosity also. To the last he uttered no reproach against the woman who had tempted his virtue and cursed his path. On the contrary, he repaid her inordinate embraces with a pure kiss of peace and reconciliation, her polluted enchantments with the sacrament of baptism, and her wandering curse by the guidance of her weary feet to their eternal rest within the gleam of the redeeming Blood.

On his return to the Grail's domain with the Sacred Lance, Parsifal was anointed King in the place of Amfortas. The chosen race had forfeited its inherited privileges, which were transferred to the child of promise. As the sin of Amfortas was reflected upon those associated with him, and in turn upon others again, so the heroic virtue of Parsifal not only rescued the Grail brotherhood from moral impotence and redeemed Kundry from her curse and spell, but was spread abroad over the face of nature itself. His first act, after assuming the majesty of the Grail sovereignty, was to extend mercy and peace to the sinful woman. His eyes were then bent in loving ecstasy upon the holy mountain, where nothing shall hurt or destroy, because on that holy day the whole earth was filled with the knowledge of the crucified Lord. The fields and meadows once cursed for man's disobedience gleamed with supernatural beauty. How pure and fresh and sweet were those fair flowers in the fragrant splendour of the spring morning! How they recalled the scenes and scents of his early childhood! What a contrast to the exotic creepers of the enchanted garden, which strove to clasp their hungry tendrils around him! How different that importunate Pagan solicitation to passionate desire from this tender appeal to the instinctive wonder and delight of innocent infancy! The land that was desolate and impassable had been made glad, the wilderness rejoiced and flourished like the lily. The glory of Libanus was given to it, the beauty of Carmel and Saron, for they have seen the glory of the Lord, and the beauty of our God.

The hermit explained the mystery. It was the magic of Good Friday which had dispelled the curse once laid upon creation. It was the Saviour's spell, the same which drew Kundry out of her long sleep and dragged home her deliverer's drifting feet to the Grail's domain. It was the charm of the heavenly Orpheus, which gathered even the animal creation round His feet. It was the magnetism of that uplifted Enchanter Who draws all men unto Him. It was the transition from nature depraved to nature redeemed, when the lion and the lamb shall lie down together, and a little child shall lead them. The arid earth had been watered with the dew of contrite sinner's tears, therefore even unconscious nature yielded up a smile of grateful recognition at the trace of its Author and Redeemer, just as the new-born infant laughs with joy upon its mother's face. The herbs which blossom here, and fast go hence, see not the uplifted Saviour on the Cross, they can but smile upon redeemed man; who, mindful of his Maker's mercy, walks tenderly on fields and flowers.

## KUNDRY.

As the object of this drama is to disclose the secret of redeeming love, we find in it a representation of that other love of desire, so commonly mistaken for the ennobling passion. For this type the dramatist has selected a woman as the embodiment of human love, and represented her as a fallen woman, in order to portray the effects of polluted passion. To express the universality of this degradation in the human race, he has created a special character in Kundry, who unites in one personality the Gundryggia of Scandinavian mythology, a wild serving-messenger of

Asgard's heroes, with the adulteress Herodias of Holy Scripture. She is a type of no one person, but displays the compound of good and evil elements common to all sinful humanity. Nameless she is called, yet answering to a hundred names. Belonging to no particular time, and yet of every age. Owning no country, and yet in every land. She represents fallen womanhood, corrupted by the distortion of that love which is the best attribute of human nature, and yet retaining the clouded reflection of her Maker's image upon the mirror of her soul.

Her metamorphic personality represents the loving emotional temperament of woman, tossed to and fro on the ebb and flow of feeling and impulse, continually alternating between selfish desire and generous self-sacrifice. She passed from derision of the Saviour to desire for salvation, from the curse of mocking laughter to a craving for penitential tears, from the slavery of destructive sin to the solicitude of helpful service. The dual nature of this personality is emphasized in the drama by her appearing under two aspects in two distinct states of existence. In the domain of the Grail she is a witch-like being, wandering and restless, yet penitent and helpful, serving the knights by way of atonement. From this her soul is drawn through the portal of a stupifying sleep into the enchanted domain of Klingsor, where she appears transformed into a woman of surpassing beauty, engaged in the diabolical work of seducing the knights of the Grail.

In her half-awakened state, in either domain, she shrinks with horror from the slavery of the enchantment.

The magic spell by which Klingsor held her bound represents the stupifying sleep of sin that blinded her spiritual vision. This illusion is the more pitiable because, as Lord Bacon says, it is born of the appetite and thirst for apparent good. But beauty had deceived her, and lust had perverted her heart. She mistook desire for love, and emotions for virtues, consuming within herself what should have been bestowed on others. While under this spell she was possessed only of the love of desire. She was blind to the fact that her spurious passion was consistent with jealousy, cruelty, and vindictiveness. She was stung to the quick at the rejection of her deluded passion, and out of jealousy at Parsifal's solicitude for Amfortas she cursed the path of the hero from whom she had craved deliverance. She imagined that her unquenchable carnal desire could be transformed into a redeeming love, and thought to gain salvation by weeping on Parsifal's bosom. As a victim of this false appetite of sensual disease she represents the animal and sensitive vitality of human nature, when predominant over the spiritual and intellectual life. Amfortas falls through spiritual pride, but Kundry through the lust of the flesh, the lust of the eyes, and the pride of life. In her mockery of our Lord she dishonoured the special function of her nature, for no woman can regard suffering without pity, or self-sacrifice without sympathy. But the seed of salvation is in her, though choked by sin and error. Her rational and intellectual faculties may be darkened and distorted, but her natural instincts and intuitions are not wholly destroyed. She does what she can, she fetches balsam from Arabia and water from the spring, and her loving service is repaid to her a thousandfold. She has loved much, and to her much is forgiven. Indeed nothing in the drama so completely overwhelms the heart as her reconciliation. Parsifal restores Amfortas with the miraculous Lance, but he delivers Kundry with pitying love alone. At his feet she kneels, with her atoning tears she washes out the stains of his wandering strife. He regenerates her with the waters of Baptism, he reconciles her with the kiss of peace, and transfigured by the radiance of the glowing Grail she yields her soul to God.

In Kundry we see a type also of the abandoned outcasts of society, despised and contemned by good and bad alike, and enslaved for the vilest ends, whose redemption may hereafter be effected by the chivalry of stainless men, who shall lead them from the servitude of Pagan enchantment into the free citizenship of the City of God.

## The Secret of Redeeming Love.

The virtue of self-renunciation, a means of closer union with God, as a release from the limitations of the flesh, and by way of expiation for sin, is a necessary condition of heroic co-operation with divine redemption. It is embodied in our Lord's words, "Whosoever shall lose his life for My sake and the gospel shall save it." This is the secret cf Redeeming Love. The heroes of this Great Renunciation are scarce, and their precepts are more often applauded than their practice is imitated. Nevertheless they have transformed the world. No miracle or wonder upon earth moves us so much. The constant tragedies of human life, the conquests, the arts and the discoveries of man, appal and astonish us for awhile, but the spectacle of self-renunciation is ever rare, and always sublime. And herein lies the power of this Mystery-Drama which reveals a Redeeming Love strong enough to arraign man's habitual self-love, and great enough to expand into eternal proportions the horizon of his moral vision. Environed for the moment by such generous loving kindness, we no longer measure life by our mean standards and limitations, since we feel "there is a wideness in God's mercy like the wideness of the sea." The fetters of selfish habit are melted by the compunction occasioned by this work of art, and the soul hovers towards heaven, from whence she sees a merciful purpose in Creation and Redemption, because all the detached and irreconcilable phenomena of life, which fret and vex her for apparent lack of aim and meaning, blend into one vast impulse of Redeeming Love.

By the power of Christ's Great Renunciation God

and man are reconciled, the dead are raised to life, the lost are found, and the wounded are made whole.

* * * * *

Such is my interpretation of the last work of a great dramatist and musician who lived to portray the mythology, the passion, and the art of humanity; and who, a little while before he died, gave this dramatic and musical expression to his own thoughts concerning the deepest and most enduring of all truths revealed by God to man.

* * * * *

"Great is the magic of Desire, greater is the strength of Renunciation."

THE END.

RIDDLE & COUCHMAN, 22, Southwark Bridge Road, London, S.E.

www.ingramcontent.com/pod-product-compliance
Lightning Source LLC
Chambersburg PA
CBHW021128020726
47500CB00003B/983
*9783337334550*